Day's End

Day's End

and other Bangla stories

Edited by

Amiya Dev

Subha Chakraborty Dasgupta

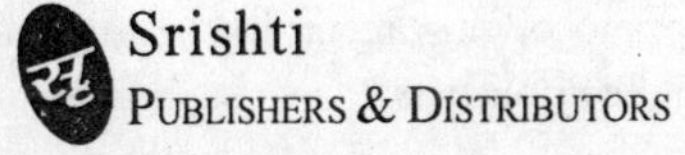

SRISHTI PUBLISHERS & DISTRIBUTORS
64-A, Adhchini
Sri Aurobindo Marg
New Delhi 110 017
srishtipublishers@yahoo.com

First published by Srishti Publishers and Distributors, New Delhi and DSA Programme, Department of Comparative Literature, Jadavpur University, Kolkata, 2003.

Rs. 250.00
ISBN 81-87075-21-X

Cover design by Shivani Babbar

Typeset in AGaramond 11pt. by Suresh Kumar Sharma at Srishti

CONTENTS

Our general policy implied that we would not overtranslate – we would retain very overtly culture specific words, if possible explain them in the body of the text itself without compromising with the communicative, semiotic and figurative properties within the syntactic constraints of the target language. Where this was not possible we took the help of certain compensatory methods, such as, notes that we placed at the end desiring minimum interference with the text. The notes provide a glossary and an explanation of very culture specific terms. In most cases, where textual function was not compromised, we retained names of plants and animals typical to India and gave their scientific names in the notes. However, we need to state that translating cultural nuances into English was often a very difficult task. Several drafts were prepared before the final version was accepted with the feeling that there can actually be no final version, and that the process remained as open-ended as before.

Translation in the Indian context is on many occasions not just a transfer from one language system into another, for within the body of the text there is often more than one linguistic register. Where this was so, our translators in most cases retained the non-Bangla words taking pains to ensure that the context explained such linguistic differences. In the case of dialects the translators had to make some kind of a compromise, preserving the tonal differences in the different dialects without taking recourse to pidgin.

When we started working with the translation projects, we realized that very little systematic work had been undertaken in

We are grateful to all authors and copyright holders for giving us permission to publish translations of the stories. We wish also to acknowledge our gratitude to Professor Manabendra Bandyopadhyay for his constant help and support in the area of translation, to Dr Suchorita Chattopadhyay, our Head of the Department, to Dr Sibaji Bandyopadhyay, Deputy Coordinator of the DSA project, to Sri Aveek Majumder for his assistance with the selection of the stories, to Sm Mohua Dey Biswas for her assistance with the preparation of the notes and to Sm Mandita Kundu for her help in typing out the manuscript. It would have been impossible to bring out this volume without the help of Dr. Mousumi Biswas and Sri Sayantan Dasgupta – but this volume is theirs as well. We also thank Professor Janet Walker, Rutgers University for reading quite a few of the stories during her stay at the department as Visiting Faculty to the DSA Programme and for offering her comments. Finally, we express our gratitude to Sm Rani Ray and the staff of Srishti for their patience and cooperation and we apologize for all the lapses that may be there in the anthology.

Amiya Dev

Subha Chakraborty Dasgupta

THE MEADOWS OF BHUSHANDI

Parashuram

Translated By Suman Ghosh

Shibu Bhattacharya lived in Peneti village. One wife, three cows, a single storied brick house, 26 homes of *yajmans*, some inherited religious property, a few families of subjects; this was enough for the smooth running of his family. Shibu was thirty two.

The little he had learnt in his childhood school, and the smattering of Sanskrit picked up from his father, had been enough to sustain both property and his *yajmans*. But Shibu's mind was not at peace. His wife Nrityakali was twenty five,had a tight, solid figure and a forceful temperament. She spared no effort in attending on her husband, but Shibu found no sap in her attentions. Little things caused quarrels between husband and wife. Shibu was exhausted after five minutes of diatribe, but Nrityakali's tongue wouldn't stop easily once it had taken off. Shibu was defeated on every occasion. His inability to tame his wife earned him sobriquets of coward, effeminate, monkey face etc., from his neighbours. This harassment indoors and outdoors alike left Shibu in no peace of mind.

One day Nrityakali learnt that her husband's character suffered aspersions. The quarrel that day scaled a new peak. Nrityakali's broom touched Shibu's back. Poor Shibu stemmed his tears of anger and anguish, spent the night as he could, and boarded a train to Calcutta at six next morning. Shibu directly went to Kalighat from Sealdah and, after a worship offering of five rupees on numerous counts, pledged thus: "O Mother Kali, let cholera take her away to you Mother, I'll offer you two goats. But this can't go on anymore. Give me one solution, so that I can start a family anew. The woman is childless, that has to be thought of as well. I swear on you Mother!"

As he returned from the temple, Shibu ate a large packetful of oil-cooked fries, half a seer of curd and half a seer of sweetmeats. Then he spent the day visiting the zoo garden, museum, Hogg's market, the High Court etc., and dined in the evening at Hotel d' Orthodox on Beadon Street over a plate of curry, two plates of roasted fowl and eight chops; he spent the night watching plays at a theatre and returned to Peneti next morning.

Mother Kali had, however, got the message wrong. As soon as he returned home, Shibu began vomiting. The doctor came, the *kabiraj* too; as a result, nothing happened. After eight hours of suffering, leaving his wife weeping at his feet, Shibu left this world.

His mind wasn't at ease in the village anymore. Shibu crossed the Ganga that very night. On the opposite bank lay Konnagar. From there he went northwards, past Rishra, past Serampore, the marketplace of Baidyabati village, the jute mills of Champdani and, six miles further away, reached the meadows of Bhushandi. The meadow stretched a long distance and was devoid of humans. There used to be a brick kiln here, so the field wasn't even, having its humps and hollows. Clumps of trees and shrubs – *assheora, ghentu, wild ol*, and *babla* – were present here and there. Shibu quite liked the place. A long abandoned heap of bricks had, on one side, a tall palm tree that shot straight up, and on the other, a leafless *bel* tree that stood with its trunk thrice doubled over. Shibu began living atop the *bel* tree as a Brahmin giant.

For those who are not well informed about spiritualism, or the science of spirits, let me explain in brief. Everyone has heard of men becoming ghosts once they die. But how do heaven, hell and rebirth fit into this theory? Here are the real facts. Agnostics don't have souls. So they are converted to hydrogen, oxygen and other gases. Those Europeans who are believers have souls, but there is no chance of rebirth. They become ghosts after death and assemble firstly at a waiting room. After an ideal existence there, their final judgement is held. The sentence passed, some go to eternal heaven, while the rest get accommodated in eternal hell. The freedom that Europeans enjoy in their lifetime is curtailed somewhat during their status as ghosts. European ghosts can't leave the waiting room without a pass. Those who have been to séance will understand how difficult it is to bring down a European ghost. There is a different system for Hindus, because we believe in everything: rebirth, heaven, hell, karma, godlessness, *tvaya Hrishikesa*, nirvana, ultimate freedom (*mukti*). The Hindu dies, and first becomes a ghost, living freely wherever he pleases, and interacting with the mortal world whenever the need arises. This is quite convenient. But this state of affairs isn't settled for long. Some are reborn in two days or four, some after ten or twenty years; some centuries later they are sent to heaven or hell for a change. This is good for their health, because a stay in heaven means bliss, while a visit to hell cleanses their sins and makes their subtle forms light and lithe, in addition, enables them to meet numerous illustrious men. But those who have the fortune to die in Kashi or have a glimpse of Pashupatinath in Nepal or Bamandev on the *ratha* or those who can leave the burden of their own sins on Lord Hrishikesh and be at peace – for them there is no rebirth, freedom is ultimate.

Two or three months have passed. Shibu lives in the same *bel* tree as before. The first few days in his new situation, in a new place, passed in mirth but now he feels quite lonely. Her tempers may have been horrid, but Nritya still tugged at his heartstrings; Shibu still felt it in his bones. Once he thought,

"Let it be, I'll settle down at Peneti". Then it occurred to him that people would say he hadn't been able to get over his wife even as a ghost. No, he would look for a suitably spiritual match.

It was a Falgun afternoon. The southern wind breezed over the winding course of the Ganga. The sun had just sunk after bobbing on the water, and the meadows of Bhushandi were full of the smell of *ghentu* flowers. New leaves had sprouted from Shibu's *bel* tree. A few ripe fruits burst plop in a distant clump of *akanda*. A few tufts of silk cotton fluttered in the wind and, shimmering like a spider's skeleton, landed on Shibu's body. A yellow butterfly flew right through his transparent self. A black beetle vroomed along, encircling him. A pair of king crows came and perched on the *babla* tree nearby. The female shut her eyes even as the male stroked her neck and, in a slurry voice, caw-aw-awed time and again. A frog having just woken up from his slumber came out of its hollow lair in the *bel* tree, looked straight at Shibu with his big eyes, and chattered away, seeming to mock at him. A school of crickets who were tuning their instruments for the evening concert, cricked forth, all together, having found resonance.

Shibu might not have his flesh and blood self, but where could death take away his mettle? Shibu's mind was lonely. The place where his heart used to be, felt full and sounded a lub dub. He remembered that atop a *shaora* tree beside the *Pituli* pool at the edge of the meadows of Bhushandi lived a female ghost. Many an evening had Shibu spotted her fishing with a *palo* in her hands. She was covered from head to foot, which she had once let slip, sighted Shibu, and bit her tongue abashed. She was elderly, her cheeks were sunken and she had lost two front teeth. She was okay for banter, but love was impossible.

A *shakcunni* had caught Shibu's eye a few times. She wore a gamcha and donned another on her head; her hair undone, she spattered cow-dung water from a large bowl down her way as she went, her legs as long as a crane's. She didn't seem too old. Shibu had tried a wisecrack but the *shakcunni* snarled at him with the rage of a cat, so Shibu had to retreat.

The one that had really stolen Shibu's heart was a *dakini*. She had taken shelter quite recently in a tumbledown house in the deserted property of Khiri Bamni, east of the meadows of Bhushandi, on the banks of the Ganga. Shibu had seen her only once, but he was mesmerised. The *dakini* was sweeping her yard with a broom of date palm. She wore white cotton. Seeing Shibu – her veil removed – she smiled for an instant, and melted into the wind. What teeth! What looks! What hue! Nrityakali had the tint of well fried sweetmeats. The *dakini's* colour was the pulp of the fry.

Shibu let out quite a deep breath and broke into song –

Aha *Radha* and *Chandravali*
Whom to retain and whom set free?

Suddenly the grounds reverberated with a piercing scream from the top of the nearby palm tree

Ca ra ra ra ra ra

Hey! Bhajua's sister, Bhaglu's daughter

Is married to a *kekara* ho……

To a *kekra* hoooo

Startled, Shibu demanded, "Who's that on the palm tree?"

"Sooty spirit here" – the answer came.

"Shibu, black ghost? Come down, pa."

A turban on his head, a lanky dark form, live-ghost slithered down lizardlike to the ground from the palm tree top, genuflected before Shibu and said, "My respects, sire Brahmin giant!"

Shibu: "Long life, son. Can you get me some tobacco?"

Sooty Spirit: "You want a chillum?"

Shibu: "There's no tobacco, let alone a chillum. Why don't you arrange for some?"

The spirit ascended and, in a little while, brought back tobacco, lighted charcoal and lit up a tobacco-holder, and gave it to Shibu. Shibu mounted the tobacco holder on a branch of *kochu*, and said as he inhaled, "So then? When did you arrive? Tell me about yourself."

The gist of the tale told by the Sooty Spirit was as follows:

His home was in the Chhapra district of Bihar. At one time, he had wife, heifers, land, property, – everything. His wife

Mungri was extremely churlish and ill-tempered, so they never got along well. One day husband and wife had a mighty quarrel over their neighbour Bhajua's sister and, after first having struck his wife on her back with a stick, the husband departed from his homeland and came over to Calcutta. That was thirty years ago. Some time later he received news that Mungri had died of pox. The husband never returned home, and never married again. He worked in different places and finally got employment as a coolie in a mill in Champdani, where he became head coolie in a few years. Sometime back, while lifting goods, an iron pulley-chain struck his head. He lay in the hospital bed for a month. Recently, having died, he had taken to living on the palm tree.

Shibu took a long, deep drag and was about to give the tobacco holder to Sooty Spirit when a cantankerous voice from the ground said, "Brother, is there any tobacco left in that holder?"

A few bricks suddenly came loose from the stack of bricks near the *bel* tree, and a figure crept out of the crevice. Short and stocky, with a face that looked as if a pair of whiskers had grown on the egg shaped body of a hookah; bald headed, with a string of rudraksha round his neck, and clad in a bell buttoned half sleeve garment, a dhoti and *taltola* slippers, it took the tobacco holder from Shibu and said, "Brahmin? I kneel before you. I had some wealth, which is buried here. I've been guarding this as a yaksha. Not much – four-five hundred. All mortage documents on stamp paper so you won't get a penny. Mind you, don't look that way or you'll have handcuffs on your hands. Pooh! Pooh!"

Shibu knew a little of Meghdut. So he asked in awe, "Sir yaksha, are you Kalidas ..."

"His brother in law. Kalidas married a cousin of my wife. He served at a salt factory in Hijli, and died a long time back. How did you know his name?"

Shibu: "How long has it been since your arrival here?"

"My arrival? Hah, hah! I've been here for, let's see, three score and a half years. I've seen so many come, and also the many who left. You came just a few days back, shooing off a few red ants and stumbling thrice before climbing the tree. I've seen everything. I've seen your interest in music; good, good. If you want to learn classical music then become my disciple. My voice may have become a trifle nasal, but even a dead elephant is worth a lakh of rupees."

"May I know sir's pre-spectral name?"

"Of course. My name is the late Noderchand Mallick, surname Basu, race kayastha, resident of Rishra, presently in this heap of bricks. Police inspector by former profession, in the area between Rishra and Bhadreswar. Have you heard of Georgette Sahib? Collector of Hooghly, – loved me a lot. Left the area's administration fully in my hands. People cried for mercy, such was Nadu Mallick's might."

"Sir's family?"

The yaksha sighed heavily and said, "Are all comforts ever destined, brother! I had a home and a family, but my wife was a shrew. What can I say, I was Nadu Mallick, the company's civil and criminal courts were in my fist and, she thrashed me on my back with a log of wood! And then went to her father's place. I could have held her under article 324 but, fearing a scandal, didn't issue an arrest warrant. But could she escape? There is the guru, there is dharma yet! Dame died in the epidemic of '47. I had no inclination to marry again. Georgette Sahib went back to Blighty, and I set up an amateur jatra troupe with money from my pension, then set about living here after I died. I had no children but I don't regret that. I would earn money, and then some ill-starred woman's spook son would be born human under my roof and inherit my property. I couldn't have taken that. Now I'm fine, and I look after my things myself, inhale the Ganga breeze and make booming noises. But let that be, you've listened to my tale, now tell me about your turpitude."

Shibu narrated his entire chronicle and introduced the Sooty Spirit. The yaksha said, "I see all of us are in the same state. There's no point feeling low, thinking of the past; let us sing and play music now. There's no drum, – no fun either. Okay, I'll strike my belly to keep rhythm. No, it tinkers. Sooty my son, apply some wet mud right here in the middle. That's right. You know the beat of four? Six meters in all; four beats, two hushed. Listen to the theorem:

Dha dha dhin dha kat ta gey
Wife beats husband everyday
Chases and chastises him
The wife is shrewd, the spouse an ass.
Grips his neck and rain on him blow after blow.
Then she clutches him, grips his tufts and turns him over upside down.
She has never been short of strength.
Never stopped shoving him left and right.
Insignificant poor creature.

Stress the 'ture'. Dhin ta tere kete gadi ghene dha. Miss the dha, and the rest is useless. My voice is failing. Sooty, light us another chillum, son"

An enterprising man can never be deterred from achieving the benevolence of his Lakshmi. So, after a lot of coaxing, the *dakini* finally agreed to be Shibu's wife. But she hadn't spoken or lifted her veil, merely signalled her consent. Today, Shibu will be married in the ghostly tradition.

Immediately after sunset, Shibu applied mud from the Ganga on his self, cleaned his sacred thread with juices of the *gaab* tree, combed his hair with cactus, and tied a ripe red fruit to his sacred tuft. He went about the bushes and got hold of a few flowers of *ghentu* and *boichi* and a few ripe *nona* and *bel* fruits. Then, in the evening, as soon as the jackals had begun their cackle concert, he made his way to the property of Khiri-Bamni.

It was still a day before full moon. Squatting in front of the *dakini*, at her yard, on a seat of kochu leaves and preparing to chant the mantra, Shibu covetously inquired, "You've got to remove your veil now.

The *dakini* removed her veil. Shibu, stupefied and terrified, said – "Oh, so you're Netto!"

Nrityakali said, "Yes my dear. So you thought you would escape my clutches by dying! It was great fun running behind the female ghost and the *shakcunni*, wasn't it?"

Shibu, "How did you come here? Was it diarrhoea?"

Nrityakali, "Diarrhoea takes my enemies. Why, wasn't there kerosene at home?"

Shibu, "That's why you look so fair. You burn gold and it gleams even more. Has your nature changed as well?"

The good deed suffered an interruption. What was the noise outside all about? As if a host of vultures were snatching and wrenching with each other. Suddenly, the she-ghost and the *shakcunni* pushed away the sleeve-lock of the thicket fence beyond the yard, and began shouting and screaming. (I've left out the nasal radicals for the benefit of the almighty beings of the printing press, the readers can apply them at will).

Ghostess, "Why should I give you my husband?"

Shakcunni: "Go and die you old hag. He is as old as your grandson!"

Ghostess: "Aha! So speaks the newlywed bride."

Shakcunni: "Go away you fish spirit, I was his wife two births ago."

Ghostess: "Away you cowdung spirit, I was his wife three births ago."

Shakcunni: "You'll die screaming, while the witch elopes with him."

Then the ghostess closed the exit and chanted, "First I'll wring your neck and then I'll feast on that witch."

Then the biting and scuffling began. As if Nrityakali alone wasn't enough, two wives from Shibu's two previous births were also present. Shibu clutched his sacred thread and chanted mantras for his own good. Nrityakali swelled in rage.

Then the voice of the yaksha sounded from the background:

Dearie, unmindful are you!
As if Shyam's lute had dragged you from the forest of bamboo
That is a jackal's cry, don't give your spouse the lie

Hearing cries of vixen, mice, with owls and doggies too, the yaksha came right up to the fence and asked, "Brother, whats going on here? Why all this noise?"

Sooty spirit said, "Hey Brahmin spirit, open the door!"

No reply from Shibu.

There was heavy pounding, but the enchanted lock didn't give way and neither did the fence. The Sooty Spirit screamed his heaveup chant.

The young man pulls, heave ho!
Just once more, heave ho!
Blast the mountain, heave ho!
Run the engine, heave ho!
Blast the boiler, heave ho!
Attention, click heels.

The roof walls, fencing and locks of the house suddenly shot up straight into the sky with a crashing sound and were thrown far off. Spotting *dakini*, that is Nrityakali, the Yaksha said, "What is this my dame! You here? With this Brahmin ghost! Shame, shame, are you off your head?" The *dakini* pulled her veil and remained seated like a log.

Sooty Spirit said, "Hey Mungri! Aren't you ashamed at all?"

Whenever I remember what took place thereafter the ink in my pen dries up. Shibu's three wives from his three previous births, and Nrityakali's three husbands from her three previous births, this double treble sparked off water-walls, forest fires and earthquakes in the meadows of Bhushandi. Ghosts, spirits, giants, and all other indigenous members of the ungodly species everywhere came down to watch the fun. Spooks, pixies, gnomes, goblins and such other clean shaven English spectres came playing pan-pipes. Genies, jans, afrids, marids and such other long bearded spirits from Kabul began a rampage. Ching,

Chang, Fachang and other whiskerless Chinese spirits practiced somersaults.

Ram, Ram, Ram. Command me, mother Chandi. Who will clear up this outlandish marital problem? Not my forte. Ghosts don't leave easily and they never let go their dues. Men's manhood, women's womanhood, ghosts' ghosthood and ghostess' ghostesshood, they understand all this perfectly. So it is my ardent request that Messers Sarat Chatterjee, Charu Banerjee, Naresh Sen and Jatin Singha discuss and find a viable solution, so that this family of ghosts is not destroyed, and so that no immoral or irregular happenings take place. If this is beyond you, then you might try a *pindadaan* ceremony at Gaya, so that they can live in peace hereafter.

Originally published as "*Bhushandir Mathey.*"

DAY'S END

Jagadish Gupta

Translated By Sayantan Dasgupta

Rati barber's house has a wonderful setting – the river Kamda to thc cast, a garden on the west, a bamboo clump in the north, and fields as far as one can see in the south. Barely has the Sun-god touched the horizon than his bright scarlet glow kisses the top of Rati's house. Rati awakes to the cackling of birds; his evening lamp under the tulsi is lit at dusk, in perfect harmony with their music as they return to their tree-homes. The bamboo clump to the north rustles in the southern breeze; it is echoed in the west – there is no end to the dance of the green. Still, Rati pays no attention to this wonder – his senses have not learnt to recognise these things. Rati is a materialist – his only interest is the master's land which he enjoys. You couldn't call Rati a bad man unless it was for his obstinacy and temper. And, unless one took Jadav Das's (the owner of the garden to the west of Rati's house), suspicions about Rati's designs on his mangoes and jackfruits to be absolutely true, Rati's character didn't have a blemish. But people took it to be true.

Many, both gentlemen and those of the rag-tag variety, have seen Rati sell mangoes and jackfruits at the village market in Ramchandrapur, some four miles away, but what is amazing is that even by interrogating him as to how he had acquired them, they couldn't get much satisfaction.

Rati has only one son, called Panchu – five years old. Rati's wife, Naraani, had put on Lord Panchugopal's amulet after having thrown three dead sons from the delivery room into the bowels of the river – then came this Panchu to her womb. So, numerous charms, amulets and talismans and various semi-divine weapons are ever alert on Panchu's body, protecting him against evil. Despite all this, though, Naraani doesn't have a grain of peace in her mind. There is no saying when the vigilant spell may begin to doze, exhausted from the never-ending battle. This flower and food offering to God may, some day, get weakened, so, everytime Panchu is out of Naraani's sight, she fears that he is no more – such is her anxiety and dread.

What Panchu, this fruit of much prayer and worship, suddenly said, immediately after waking up one morning, was as incredible as it was frightening. Naraani was walking him towards the field, Panchu was walking quietly alongside when he suddenly looked up at his mother's face and said, "Ma, the crocodile will take me today."

Naraani started and asked, "What's that?"

"Yes, Ma, the crocodile will take me today."

"How did you know?"

"That – I don't know," said Panchu.

Though Naraani had been startled by the boy's terrible words, her apprehension subsided soon upon reflection and she was able to heave a sigh of relief. Panchu has often spoken incomprehensible things; he had once claimed to have seen an owl one evening sitting on their roof and roaring in laughter. On another occasion, he had seen a giant tortoise and its baby standing upright and dancing in the courtyard. Panchu had a knack of saying such crazy things regularly – the madcap!

Rati listened to his wife's report of what Panchu had said and glared and berated him loudly. In this connection, he was reminded of Adhar Bakshi of their village, now dead. Adhar Bakshi was to go on a boat journey the next day. That evening, the sight of his shadow in the misty moonlight had made him scream. He had jumped and pointed at his shadow and had asked repeatedly, "Who's that? Who's that?" Nobody had the courage that evening to look him straight in his bloodshot, unblinking eyes. After a lot of effort, his fears were allayed. But his boat did not come back, neither did he. A certain wise man had called Rati to his side that evening and had told him, "It doesn't look good, Rati. It's an omen of death. Only a madman or one whose end is near, has such hallucinations."

He had been proved right, word for word. So, Rati assumed

a strict countenance and took his son to task. "Mind! If you dare say that again I'll snap a green twig on your back."

It was early Aashar. The river had grown and submerged the shallows and was lapping up the soil of the steep bank with a splashing sound; the clear and still water had become muddy and rough. Yet there was no reason for fear. This river, the Kamda, its two banks and its water were ever known to them; this river was not a bloodthirsty ogress – no, never. She was loving like the suckle-giving mother, she had even brought to their village huts' doors, the cool and sweet water of the mountains. She was not to be feared.

When it was time to bathe, Rati called Panchu and said, "Come! Let's go and bathe." Afraid of being caned, Panchu made no protest and ran to his mother; he held on to her back, put his arms round her neck and said, "I won't bathe today, Ma."

"But, why?"

"I'm scared."

Naraani carried her son in her lap outside the house and said, "Panchu won't take his bath today".

"Why? What's wrong?" Rati asked, raising his eyebrows.

"Nothing!"

"Then?"

"Doesn't want to, why not let it be today?"

Rati became sterner and said, "No, he should be disabused

of his wrong notion. I related the matter to the Babu, and he began to laugh. Not only did he laugh, there were so many others – and they all laughed."

Rati had narrated the boy's words as he sat in front of the village landlord, Mr Choudhury, while polished his razor on leather. Not only had the Babu laughed, but none of those present had been able to check their laughter. A crocodile in the Kamda? What can be funnier than this? Choudhurybabu had said, "No, you take him with you and give him a bath. If the crocodile takes anyone, it will take you ..."

Rasik Poddar had taken words out of the Babu's mouth and said, "Babu's right. You'll provide it its food." Haladhar had moved to a side and was dragging on a clay pipe. Exhaling a mouthful of smoke, he said, "Rati, you are Babu's subject. So ignorant! And you are a barber by birth, no less!"

Irritated by these irksome taunts and remembering Adhar Bakshi's hallucination of a similar nature and his consequent death, Rati had returned home determined to take Panchu to the river that day.

Naraani told Panchu, "Go, my son. Have a bath. A grown-up man is going with you. What do you have to fear?" So saying, she kissed Panchu affectionately and put him down. She prayed silently that he would live to be a thousand years.

On other days, Panchu would be fidgety when he was being massaged with oil. Today, he stood still and didn't protest at all. He took his father's *gamchha* (towel) and followed him to the river.

The bank had been cut, and a sloping path leading right to the river cleared to help bathers go up and down.

Rati climbed down to the edge of the water, and then suddenly stopped. He felt strangely scared. The muddy, expansive, ripple-less mass of water lay in a terrifying silence, shining brilliantly in the mid-day sun like a sharpened scimitar. The uncontrollable current raced on in great speed, soundless, foamless, almost as if you couldn't see it. It was as if all the unbridled, ravaging power of Shiva, the one who captured Ganga in his locks, was arrested in the unperceivable form of this silent, solemn motion – the beloved river had never appeared so utterly merciless before. It looked so frightening from the outside. Who knew what violence lurked inside its hidden womb with fangs bared! Rati shivered. Fearfully, he looked as far as he could see in front, to his right, to his left – there was not even a bubble anywhere on the surface of the silent, motionless river. The stretch of sand on the other side passed between two villages and disappeared into the horizon; the point where it met the sky was like a smoky, hazy, never-ending line. At some places far away, clumps of grass had come up, punctuating the naked, empty whiteness of the never-ending mass of sand with green dots. The two banks of the river were lonely and quiet. Rati kept on musing.

Suddenly Panchu let out a scream of terror and ran to Rati.

He held him tight and said. "What is that?"

Rati, too, had seen the thing that had frightened Panchu – an ugly aquatic animal had whooshed its way to the surface and had immediately somersaulted and disappeared into the depths again.

Rati smiled at Panchu's scared face and said, "That's a dolphin. It was after a fish."

"Why, Baba?" asked Panchu.

"Because it's hungry." There was no end to Panchu's amazement when he was told that they even kill big carps and eat them – it's so dark inside the water how do they hunt out their prey?

This insignificant incident and the opportunity to laugh that it offered, drovc away Rati's fearful stupor. Then he remembered that nobody from his village had ever seen a crocodile in the Kamda, nor had any such rumour reached the village from distant lands. Then what was there to fear?

Lest he should suddenly tumble into deep water, Rati extended his foot gingerly and waded in up to his knees. He pulled Panchu to his knees, used one hand to hold him by the shoulder, and the other hand to scrub him. He pushed him in by his shoulders, then pulled him up, wiped him and rubbed his hair dry and sent him home.

Rati came back and said with a smile, "Where are you, Panchu?" "I'm eating, Baba," replied Panchu from inside the kitchen.

"So, the crocodile hasn't taken you, has it?"

Panchu, looking at his mother with a smile on his face, said, "No."

"Now, finally, my son is smiling," said Naraani.

When Naraani woke from her nap that evening and went to the verandah, a number of children, all around Panchu's age, disappeared at lightning speed. What Naraani saw when she came to investigate the reason behind this sudden flight, was like nothing she had ever seen. Naraani was so shocked that she sat down, cradling her head in her arms. "Panchu," she yelled.

Panchu's friends had probably sprinted back home, but, though Panchu had started to run with his friends, he had failed to get out of the compound. On hearing Ma's call, he emerged from the shelter of the kitchen and lethargically went and stood in front of her. The sight of her son made Naraani burn in rage.

It was like this –

When Naraani was sleeping, Panchu and his companions had filched a jackfruit from the house and had broken it and started to eat. But, since they did not know the art of breaking into a jackfrut, the sticky liquid had bathed him through and through – and then, out of joy, he had also rolled in the dust of the courtyard. So, it was only natural that the sight of her son would make the mother burn in rage.

Panchu, the only one of the mischief-makers to have been

caught, sidled up to his mother, faced her unforgiving eyes and began to cry. Panchu barely escaped getting beaten up; he had, after all, been tortured by fear throughout the day. But his unnecessary cries and Naraani's enraged shouts roused Rati from sleep. He came out and stretched himself and said, as hoarse as the son's voice was his, "What the matter?"

"It's my last rites, what else – the son has learnt to steal and eat jackfruit," said Naraani. So saying, she looked at Rati in such a way as if to imply that stealing and eating jackfruits was a common practice among the male of the species.

Rati raised his eyebrows and said, "Stop it! No more shouting! I will go and get him washed. That will do, won't it?" So saying, he stepped down to the courtyard.

Panchu had a toy pot in his hand. With that in hand, the weeping, guilty Panchu walked to the river in front of his father. Rati pushed him into the water, scrubbed and washed him thoroughly and, pulled him up again. After climbing back part of the way, Panchu suddenly stoppped and asked, "Baba, my pot?"

Both of them looked back – the pot lay at the edge of the water.

"Let me get it back?" beseeched Panchu.

"Go," said Rati.

Panchu had crouched down and picked up his pot and turned back when two huge eyes silently floated up on the surface of the water near him.

The next moment, there was a flash in the water; the tail did a sudden turn and moved at lightning speed – in the twinkling of an eye, Panchu was drawn into the water, and had disappeared. It didn't take much time for the tongue-stuck, shut-eyed Rati to get over his startled state. In a moment, his loud, incessant screams drew a crowd to the banks.

When Panchu was seen again somewhere near the opposite bank, he was in the crocodile's mouth – motionless. The crowd raised a cry. Panchu's face, yellow in death, caught the sun's last blood-red rays and began to glow. The crocodile made an offering of its food to the sun and disappeared again.

Only Panchu's mother didn't see that sight. She lay unconscious.

(Originally published in Bangla as *'Dibash-er Seshe'*)

SIDE BY SIDE

Banaphool

Translated by Damayanti Chakrabarty

I am just exhausted – sitting around, lying down, reading newspapers, playing cards, chatting idly or gossiping – sick of it all. There's no peace of mind. The real reason is that I have no money. I did all that I could have done. I got through my examinations. I sent many applications for jobs, even spent some days as an insurance agent, but all in vain. Of course, there are many things still left for me to do. I've often planned to open a stationery or a grocery shop, or at least a betel-leaf and *bidi* stall, but ... oh, these pestering flies are so irritating! The moment I lie down a little, they come and sit right in the corner of my eyes. So many flies and such sultry weather! I can hardly settle down and think. I sit up. On such an oppressive afternoon it is troublesome even to sit and think. And if you lie down there are the flies. If I had some money I would have sprayed fly-repellent and would have settled down to think for sometime. Perhaps you are all laughing at me and wondering, "Oh, what a thoughtful man!"

There is no thought as simple or as intricate as that dealing with the means of livelihood. It is this thought that is plaguing me day and night. I am not thoughtful, but thought-ridden.

... I have made up my mind. I will go to Calcutta. I'll try my best in Calcutta. I should not waste away in this village. If I have to set up a shop, Calcutta will certainly be the best place. I may even get a job. You can never tell. So long I have been staying at home and making applications. If I go round offices, it is not unlikely that I will land up with something. To go to Calcutta is the right decision.

Next morning I set out with my father's silver hubble-bubble. I will pawn it and get some money. To go to Calcutta without money makes no sense. At the mention of 'silver hubble-bubble' don't presume that I am the son of a rich landowner. None of that. My father was a man of refined tastes and perhaps that was why he could leave nothing behind. I got about ten rupees by pawning the hubble-bubble. I also had about ten rupees with me. So, I set out.

Two

I came to stay at the house of a distant relative. The relationship was so complex that it was difficult for me to decipher what my ties with Bikashbabu were. This Bikashbabu was actually my mother's sister's daughter's aunt-in-law's nephew's cousin-in-law's own brother-in-law. One had to make elaborate calculations to figure out what the relationship was. I did not go into all that trouble and told him at the first sight, "Dear brother, can you place me?" Brother most surely did not. Nevertheless, he replied, "It's been a long time, isn't it? That's why – I mean – aren't you coming from Bansbede?"

I realized that there must be one branch of his family living at Bangsabatika as well. I explained, "Oh, no! It seems you could not place me. That's not surprising. I am from Bankura. Actually we live in the very interior of Bankura. Now, I am your ..." I rattled off the complex formula of relations which I had learned by heart from mother and, concluded, "So you happen to be our Hemanta's brother-in-law. My own relative living in one of the alleys of Calcutta – we hardly ever meet. This time I thought, let's go and see how our Bikash is getting along."

Bikashbabu glanced at my discoloured trunk and tattered bedding on the porter's head and asked, "Are you going to stay here?"

"Not for long – just a few days."

"Oh, I see!"

The porter put down the bedding and other baggage, took the money and went away.

A little later I noticed brother Bikash take his meal, change and leave. I kept on sitting alone, silently. However, I could not remain undisturbed for long. A group of boys and girls of different sizes came and surrounded me. Some demanded, "Lozenges!" Some said, "I want kites!" Some put their hands inside my pockets without wasting a word. I have a mole at the tip of my ear – some became happily engrossed with it. Only children can get intimate within such a short span of time! I was compelled to go out.

Three

Three days passed by. I had come to Calcutta almost ten years ago to pursue my studies. Now, I looked around but found no acquaintances. All my classmates had moved away. The professors were all new. The boarding house where I used to stay earlier was now a dyeing-cleaning shop. No one recognized me – I too recognized none. After sauntering about a bit, I had to return to brother Bikash's place. The next three days passed in the same manner. I met Bikashbabu briefly only in the mornings. He used to hustle about the entire morning so that he didn't get late. He would go out in the mornings with a *gamchha*, return from the market, put down the things he bought and immediately start applying oil on his body. Hurriedly rubbing his head and body with oil, he would rush under the tap for his bath and from there order his wife, "Serve the rice. Are you listening, my dear ...? I'll be late ... it's already a quarter to nine ... it takes some time to reach there as well ..." Then he would gulp his meal down and rush out. He returned at ten at night, sometimes at eleven. Thus I got little opportunity to become familiar with Bikashbabu. I found him a terribly busy person. And I felt jealous of brother Bikash, seeing him going out to work everyday, remaining busy throughout the day and sleeping soundly at night. Couldn't I take the help of brother Bikash? If he tried, he would surely be able to land a job for me.

Four

The next day I joined him.

Just when he had finished his meal and was rushing out, I said, "Brother, I will also go out with with you."

"With me? Why?"

"I want to tell you something. I mean ..."

"Then come along. Don't hang around, I am getting late, that fellow will reach there."

I went out at once.

While walking down the street Bikashbabu asked, "What is it you want?"

"I mean ..." I wondered how to broach the subject.

"I cannot lend you money, let me warn you right away."

"No, no, it's not a matter of money ... all right, I will tell you on the tram."

"Oh no, I am not taking the tram. I'll walk."

"That's all right. Come, I'll also walk with you. How far?"

"Eden Gardens."

"Your office is at the Eden Gardens? Which office?"

Bikashbabu looked at me smilingly and asked, "Who told you anything about an office?"

"Then?"

"Oh God, so you thought that I go to an office everyday?"

"Where do you go then?"

Bikashbabu hesitated a little and said, "I run away."

I stared at him speechlessly. Bikashbabu went on to explain, "My father had left some money in fixed deposit. I maintain my family with the interest of forty rupees earned on it. I couldn't get a job even after trying continuously for three years. Yet I had secured a first class in my M.A. Keep moving, we're getting late – if that chap reaches before me, I will not get the bench."

We silently walked along, side by side, for sometime. Bikashbabu spoke again, "Please don't divulge this secret at home. They know that I am working as an apprentice in a big firm without any salary. My salary will be fixed later. That makes her cook the early meals for me."

We again walked, side by side, for a while. Once again Bikashbabu said, "I run away, don't you see? It's impossible to stay at home with that flock of children around. They are always demanding something or the other. Buy me flutes! Get me lozenges! Buy me dolls! The boy next door has got a red shirt. Get me one like that! The wife also makes a lot of fanciful demands! I just escape, understand?"

And we are quiet for sometime.

Bikashbabu again resumed smilingly, "There's trouble if I stay at home, see? That night I returned home and heard that my youngest son had fallen and had fractured his skull. His nose had bled profusely as well. Had I been at home, I would have had to rush out to get a doctor, even with borrowed money. It's a relief that I was not present. Please move a bit faster – there is a bench in the shade of a tree in Eden Gardens. I spend the whole day lounging on that – you see – if I'm late, another chap grabs the place – see?"

We walked side by side with hurried steps.

The vacant bench in the Eden gardens should not be allowed to slip away.

(Originally published in Bangla as *Pashapashi.*)

BIRTH OF A GOD

Shibram Chakraborty

Translated By Sayantan Dasgupta

I often stumble on my way out from my house. The rock emphatically gives notice of its presence as soon as I take the first step. I've been wondering for quite some time how to deal with it.

There wasn't the least bit of haste on my part to get out of the house that day and, I definitely did not have any intention of scrambling down in such a tearing hurry. But my encounter with the rock so rudely accelerated my pace that I was left unable to check myself even though I saw the motorcar rolling in from the other direction. But what luck, the driver was alert – otherwise!

I've been musing right since that day how to deal with it. That a small piece of rock would present itself thus, as an adversary in the middle of my life's path, I could never have imagined. Besides, what is disconcerting is the fact that this is gradually turning into a life-and-death matter for me, for I cannot hope that racing motorcars will be so indulgent of my transgressions forever.

That is why I tell myself, let it be this way or that; it's either him, or me. It is a matter of grave doubt if I will be around for long even if he is. Thus, since it is my sticking around that is, at least to me, the more desirable of the two, I found it necessary to get hold of a spade one morning and get down to work.

A boulder, somewhat on the larger side, embedded in the earth; only a small part of it peeped out from the ground. When, after a lot of effort, I succeeded in fully uprooting it, I wiped the sweat off my brow and looked around to see myself surrounded by a mob. I understood that it was people's silent and not-so-silent encouragement that had lent power to my arms.

Looking at them questioningly, I asked, "Do any of you want this rock?" A ripple of excitement ran through the crowd, but there was no telling if any of them was interested in the offer. So, I announced again, "If you want it, you can have it. You need not hesitate. If someone takes it, I will deem my efforts worthwhile – fruitful – and it goes without saying that I will feel very happy."

Someone stepped out from one end of the group and asked "Why were you digging this up? Did you have a dream, or what?"

I looked askance at the man and then said, shaking my head, "No, it's not what you're thinking."

I set the rock down in a secure corner by the side of the road. But, the gentleman didn't believe me, it seemed; he shook his head absent-mindedly a couple of times, and then asked again, "You really didn't? Some divine order or some such thing?"

"Nuth-thing!"

Having thus thoroughly deflated the gentleman's enthusiasm, I came upstairs and asked Ma to prepare two cups of tea. Both, for myself. My struggle with the rock had turned my limbs stone-heavy. I was totally exhausted.

After this incident, I sometimes meet the boulder as I go out, or as I return home; sometimes, when I'm preoccupied, I don't. By this time, I have been able to bring myself to forgive its transgressions from the bottom of my heart, for it no longer has the ability to engineer my fall. It has lost that divine power. A certain rapport has built up between us now, one could say. And then suddenly one day, I saw that the stone had got its grace back; the dust and grime had vanished and a divine sparkle had appeared. Clearly, it was one of those people who sprinkle water on the road with their hosepipes every morning and evening whose benevolent look had fallen on him. I was pleased to see the improvement in his physiognomy.

"So, what do you say?"

On being thus confronted with a sudden question from behind, I turned around. It was that inquisitive gentleman from the other morning.

"Don't tell me you have been standing guard here from that day itself? Or, is it that you've received some divine order?" I asked.

"No, no, of course not! It's just that this is the route I usually take!"

The gentleman was somewhat embarrassed, but managed to get over his discomfiture in no time.

"The stone's still doing okay, I see. Won't somebody take it, what do you think?"

The way he asked the question made it seem as if the object, that was lying on the road, was more priceless than any other that could be found in the whole of the land and, as though unseen enemies were hatching a grave plot at this very moment to steal it, as if they are only waiting with their greedy arms outstretched for an opportunity to grab it. I reassured him, saying, "His Majesty's government has surely misunderstood your rivals and has invited them over as special guests to the madhouse at Ranchi and has arranged for their hospitable stay there. Since you are the only one who remains free, I see no reason for you to worry."

He smiled a little and said, "You and your ideas! Look, somebody has been here to worship it."

I scrutinised it carefully – yes, he's right! Things were different when I saw it in the morning; somebody in the meantime, had smeared the rock with *sindoor.*

I expressed joy at the development – Excellent! At last, it has picked up another admirer!

I'd expected the man to be thrilled at the respect the stone was being accorded, but he was clearly quite jealous. He knit his brows and said, "That's just what I'm afraid of! I hope that admirer doesn't manage to slip off with it!"

When I got up the next morning, there was no trace of the stone. I was puzzled at its sudden disappearance. Who had taken it? Where was it now? Several such questions rose up unbidden, and no credible, convincing answers were available. That the man who took this route regularly would be highly disheartened by the absence of the stone was not hard to imagine. I actually felt myself sympathising with him as I thought thus, but, then, who knew if it were not the handiwork of that inquisitive philosopher himself!

Weeks have passed. I am walking past the trees at the mouth of the lane – O *Hori*! So, the stone has been brought here! The narrow end of the rock has been buried near the base of the trees in such a way that the neatly-rounded, polished, smooth end sticking out might make one mistake it for a *Shiva linga*. One must appreciate the ingenuity of the man responsible for this. Flowers, *bel* leaves and *aatapchaal* lie scattered all around the rock. It is evident that those who, take this road in the morning to go and bathe in the Ganga, thirsting for divine blessings, have facetiously taken resort to this golden opportunity to increase their chances of bagging salvation for themselves. Anyway, he is reigning here quite regally – there is, thus, no reason for anybody to have any worries about its future, which is evidently quite bright.

I was truly pleased at the enhancement in the boulder's status. It was I who had given him freedom one day; now let him dole out salvation to all. His glory– isn't it my glory as well? It was I who had brought him into this world. Thus, I felt a certain amount of the pride which comes with fatherhood. I wished him well from the bottom of my heart.

I have wondered occasionally whether or not to appraise that man of his god's whereabouts. We have run into each other occasionally, but he hasn't broached the topic of the stone. I had imagined that the disappearance of the stone would make him despondent, but, on the contrary, he looked rather contented. Why do something that would get him all agitated again once he has managed to overcome pangs of separation of such great magnitude,

Sometimes, I take the path past the *aswatha* tree, while returning home. I observed that the respect the boulder commands was increasing by the day. One day, I saw that a few *sanyasis* had set up camp there. Thanks to the smell of *ganja* and the *Bom Bom* chants, it's sheer torture for one's olfactory and auditory perceptions to be walking that way. Now that the *sanyasis* are there, it won't be too long before the bhakts arrive, and the superabundance of bhakti, will take the form of a mandir reaching into the heavens, complete with clay-and-wood idols et al in the not-too-distant future. The god would then gain in prestige and the provision allowing for the collection of dues on his behalf from the masses on a Permanent Settlement-like basis would then become effective.

Within a few days of this, I had to leave for Champaran to spend a few months there in connection with a sugar factory. I could take the path that went past the *aswath* tree; I thought, let me see before I leave, how things are. What I had expected had happened – the arrival of the *sanyasis* had heralded an assembly of *bhakts*. The crux of what I could gather by standing there and listening in on their conversations was that the thing here was *Trilokeswar* Shiva, Lord of the three Worlds. He had forced his way up and emerged from the nether regions, he was immeasurable and limitless. Therefore, if he is to be worshipped with the respect he deserves, a temple must be dedicated to him.

For a moment, I felt like announcing to everybody the truth about the limitlessness of *Trilokeswar* Shiva, but I didn't have a life insurance policy and I was aware how fearsome a form *bhakti* could assume; besides, there was not too much time left for my train. Considering all this, I desisted. I realised I had done well not to inform that gentleman, for, though, as far as I could understand, his intention was to take the boulder and establish it as a deity through his own efforts, it was difficult to say whether he would have been more delighted or disheartened to learn that the rock had, by dint of its own calibre, already earned that position without waiting for the bhakt to lift a finger.

When I returned after a few months, the crossing near the *aswath* tree could hardly be recognised. A modest temple had made its appearance, the din raised by the *sankho-ghanta* made life difficult for the ears, and one had to wade through a crowd of *bhakts* to reach one's destination. But that is not what I'm concerned with. What surprised me most was the presence of another; not just presence, but his total physical transformation. That man in the temple campus – that earliest, first and most genuine worshipper! He could hardly be recognised behind the saffron, *tilak* and *rudraksha* beads.

"What is this?"

I took the onus of starting the conversation.

"This humble man is Lord Shiva's servant, my lord," the man answers self-effacingly.

"That, I can see. A nice little business, this is – one that doesn't need any investment. So, this is what you had on your mind when you were keeping such strict vigil on the stone?"

It was probably my realisation that his affection towards this piece of rock was false and, not in the least, unselfish, that suddenly made me so angry with him. I become very rude.

He stopped his ears up with his fingers and said "You shouldn't speak like that. Why do you say 'stone', *Moshai*? Sri Vishnu!! A veritable deity! *Trilokeswar* Shiva!"

He addresses a *namoshkar* in that direction.

I burst into laughter. “It has no end, right?”

This time, he’s a little disturbed. “That’s what everybody says.”

“What do you yourself say? They say that however much you dig below it, you’ll still see that Shiva linga; it’s like a tube well – it goes down all the way. But, what do *you* think?”

“I don’t know! I guess that’s the way it is!”

“Why don’t you try and find out one day how far the roots go down, huh?”

The man winced and said, “Why say all that? It’s sin to say such things! Our Lord sees and hears everything; he’s all-powerful!

“You don’t say! How powerful is he, eh?”

“Take this, for instance! There’s such a severe outbreak of pox in Calcutta this year! Not vaccine, not anything else, nothing’s working.”

“H-uh, what is that? An epidemic, you say? But I didn’t know of it!”

“You only have to take a peek at the newspaper to see how many people are dying. There is no laxity on the part of the Corporation as far as the administering of vaccine is concerned, but still, in every single ward ... but nobody in our *paara* has been affected so far, thanks to the deity. And, we haven’t been vaccinated either, remember? We’ve just had the Lord’s *channamrita*. If that's not powerful, then what is?"

There was no time to mull over how to respond to this. I had once, earlier, suffered terribly due to this disease and managed to survive with a lot of difficulty, and so, I was, by this time, least interested in explanations of Lord *Triloknath*'s power and glory. "I must go and take the vaccine right now. I'll come and chat some other day." So saying, I began to hurry in the direction of the Medical College without a moment's delay.

On the way, I met a certain friend of mine. Pausing, he asked me, "*Arre*, where are you rushing to in such a hurry?"

"To get myself vaccinated."

"But, the vaccine's falling flat on its face. Vaccination is bull shit! Instead, why don't you go and take a dose of King Company's Variolinum-200? One more dose next week, then another one, and you're home and dry. You often see vaccination fail, but Variolinum, never!"

"Oh, is that so? I didn't know that!"

"How will you? You have only learnt cutting and stitching. Do you people have any faith in anything else? I've started practicing homoeopathy, so I know."

"All right, then that's what I'll have."

I went to King Company and forced a dose of Variolinum-200 down my throat. Aah! At last, I felt reassured.

Shortly after this, several funeral processions passed by that way, one after the other – surely, they must have all died of pox? How terrible, even the thought of it sent shivers down one's spine. Who knew how many millions of germs and microbes were proliferating into the atmosphere? Variolinum had hardly reached the bloodstream and, already, these deadly germs must have started their work! My limbs grew heavy and my whole body began to feel fatigued; I was even finding it difficult to breathe the dangerous air.

On a tiny piece of paper stuck on the wall, I saw the name of some famous *kabiraj* who was known to specialise in treating pox. I've tried homoeopathy – why not give *kabiraji* a try as well? Survival, that's what matters; doesn't matter what it costs. The first thing I saw when I reached the advertised address was a group of people ceremoniously grinding something in a huge *sheel.* As soon as I told the *kabiraj* about my condition, he pointed at them and said, "There! It's being ground! The root of the *kantikari* – it has to be ground and then eaten. There's nothing else that prevents pox so effectively, *Moshai*!"

So, I partook of the stuff as he directed, and climbed onto a rickshaw. All strength seemed to have deserted my body. I felt drowsy and a little feverish; those were the early indications of pox, people said. Returning home, I told my mother, "I won't have anything today, Ma. I'm not feeling well."

Anxiety writ large on her face, Ma said, "What's wrong with you, my child?"

"Nothing as yet! Will happen, I think! Pox."

"*Balaai shaat!* Why do you say such things? Here, tie this piece of *hortoki* round your arm. I've had this round my arm for 30 years. So many pox victims I have nursed. Thanks to this (touchwood), not even measles ... Here, you take this."

Ma pulled the amulet off her arm. "Not once did you catch it in 30 years – serious? Where is it – let me have it, then. Why didn't you tell me all this time? What will this single piece do? The disease has advanced quite a bit. Give me a whole *hortoki.* Hopefully, that will do the trick."

I did tie the *hortoki* round my arm, but towards evening, I was feeling quite feverish. I observed myself carefully in the mirror. It seemed a few blisters had appeared on the face, too. Must be pox. There's no escape, then. I called Ma and showed her.

Ma said, "No, you only have a few pimples."

I said, "Uh-huh! It's definitely pox, the disease they call 'the Mother's blessings."

Ma said, "Don't utter such inauspicious words. It's nothing. You've been sitting at home the whole day – go and take a walk."

Can one walk around with such a worry in one's head? That man was saying that they were all okay, thanks to the *charanamrita* they were drinking. Perhaps I should also have some. Maybe there's some medicinal power to *channamrita*, who can tell? Huh, the things he says! That is purely an accident. Is all of Kolkata safe from disease? Besides, mental strength engenders the strength to fight disease; that, too, they can bank on. But where will I find the faith to worship that little piece of stone as a god?

I should have taken the vaccine in the morning, rather than go through all this rigmarole. Maybe, that would have helped. Should I go now and get myself vaccinated? If you take the vaccine, the pox doesn't appear in its deadly form, I've heard; at best it appears as *haam*, as measles. And there's not that much to fear as far as measles is concerned – it happens to kids, *humesha*, ever so often. Okay, to the Medical College I'll go.

As I was walking past the *ashwath* tree after having got myself vaccinated, the words the man had spoken in the morning came back to me. He was right, come to think of it! Really, there's nothing to be done after a certain point; you have to accept defeat to the mysterious and the unexplained. Here I am alive, today, but if I die of pox tomorrow, where do I go? Those words of Shakespeare – no, they're not exactly trash. How much do we know of this world, this life, the heavens, and what lies beyond? How much can our science explain? However much we talk about science, in the end, in front of the unknown, we have no answer.

Walking past the mandir, I addressed my prayers to Triloknath. I prayed silently – Baba, forgive my foolishness, save me from the clutches of this epidemic.

After having walked on some distance, I turned back again.

No, there's no sense in trying to cheat a god. I felt the blisters on my face with my fingers. Pimples? Or, is it pox? This time, I prostrated myself on the ground and did my *pranaam*. "Joy Baba Triloknath!" I said. "Save me, Baba!"

I stood up and surveyed my surroundings – I haven't been seen, have I?

(Originally published in Bangla as *Debotaar janma*)

BRINE

Syed Mujtaba Ali

Translated By Sayantan Dasgupta

That same old Goaland-Chandpur ship. My relationship with it is thirty years old. Even if somebody were to blindfold me, I could still grope my way to where the water tap was, the tea-and-paan shop was, or the place where they kept the chicken coops was – so well did I know my way around. Yet, I'm not a *khalasi*, a sailor on the ship; I'm a mere passenger.

Everything else has changed during these thirty years of our acquaintanceship; only the dispatch steamer group hasn't changed. There was always a difference between the deck of one ship and that of another, between the cabin of this ship and the cabin of that ship – there still is – but all ships smell the same wet and musty, and the smell that overwhelms all others is that of chicken curry being cooked. I have often wondered if the ship itself is not a giant chicken and if its curry is not being cooked in its own insides. You get this smell as soon as you reach any station – Chandpur, Narayanganj, Goaland. The old smells, sights and perceptions were all still there, but I noticed that the crowd was not what it used to be.

I had finished a well-laid-out lunch and was reclining in the deckchair and gazing at the distant horizon. Poetry doesn't come easily to me, so my eyes don't register natural beauty until Rabi Thakur points it out. That is why I prefer the gramophone box to the moonlight. I was just planning to get the portable when my eyes alighted on a crumpled copy of the periodical called *Desh*. If she became further 'soiled' at the hands of another in her master's absence, her 'husband' would probably not mind too much.

A new writer going by the pen-name, Rupadarshi, has come out with a sensitive story on *khalasis*. The lad obviously has talent; otherwise, he wouldn't have been able to say so many things so neatly. Nor would he have been able to record all those scandalous tales. And, look at me – the thought of writing a leave application terrifies me. But, what this chap has written, is it all true? If it is, then, why don't the *khalasis* take up arms against the grave injustice? Hunh! What a stupid thought! That's like the greenhorn amateurs of Sylhet and Noakhali taking on the professionalism of the crafty Englishmen – me and my ideas!

It looks like the *Mejo Serang*, the Second Officer of the ship, is on leave today. He patrols the decks in a silk lungi, *chikan*-worked kurta and an embroidered *kisti-toupee.* Now and then, he looks at me through the corner of his eye, the small fry in Dispatch and the whale in a man o' war – they're both fish, after all – so, why not ask him how much of what Rupadarshi has written is real and how much he has woven out of his fantasies.

I cleared my throat and asked, "O *Serang* saheb, the ship's not running late, is it?"

The man answered my query and said, "Please don't address me so formally. I haven't seen you more than once or twice, but your *abba* saheb and your elder-brother sahebs have done this poor man much *mehrbaani* – I'm obliged to them."

This pleased me. "Where do you come from?" I asked. "Why don't you sit down if you have the *fursaat*?"

He sat down on the deck with a thud.

"What are you doing?' I asked. Get a stool. These days ..." I didn't finish; nor did the officer bring a stool. We got down to learning about each other. We didn't avoid talking of our happiness and sorrows – it was someone from home, after all. Finally, I got my *mauka,* my opportunity, and read him the whole of 'Rupadarshi Darshan'. He listened to the whole thing with rapt attention just the way his farmer kinsmen at home would listen to books read out to him, and then let out a never-ending sigh.

He raised one hand to his forehead in a gesture meant to invoke Allah and said, "You talk of *insaaf,* huzoor, but where is *insaaf* in this world? The people Khuda has given wealth are the ones who are the most unjust. Besides, can anybody explain Khudatalai's sense of *insaaf*? You knew Samiruddin, didn't you – the one who spent many years in America and earned a lot of money?"

The mention of America rang a bell. "From Chautali Pargana, I think, no from ... no, from somewhere thereabouts ..."

"He was from my own village, Dhalaichhara," said the *Serang*. "Few have earned the kind of money he earned abroad. We had signed and taken up our jobs together at Kidderpore – same day, same place."

"What happened to him?" I asked. "I don't seem to remember."

"Listen, then ..."

"The piece huzoor read out – everything it says is very true. But the kind of murderous experiences working on a ship involves, particularly at the beginning of your career is something that cannot be narrated by someone who has not been inside this *gehnnum* himself. Have you ever noticed how much the man, who stands beside the boiler and shovels the coal, hour after hour, sweats? – on this very ship, where both sides are open and where the strong Padma breeze can enter and make an exit with relative ease. It's a *behesht*, a Paradise. And inside the womb of the ship, in the engine room, every side is closed; no air can enter from any direction. And, how big the boiler rooms of those h-u-u-g-e ten-twelve-fourteen thousand ton ships are, and how hot it is there! Can this be even imagined by one who hasn't experienced it himself? We have grown up among the ponds, tanks, rivers and in the free air and, we suddenly find ourselves face-to-face with these bl-a-a-ck h-u-u-u-ge devilish machinery in this *gehnnum*."

"Initially, everybody throws a fit after joining work. They are then dragged upstairs and laid out under the running tap. When they come to, they are fed fistfuls of salt; a person cannot live if all the salt of his body drains out."

"Or, you will see, someone is shovelling the coal perfectly into the boiler, when suddenly, without any warning, he'll throw his shovel aside and begin to hurtle his way through staircase after staircase, intent on jumping off the open deck into the sea. He's lost his head in the terrible heat – in ship parlance, this is called going emokh".

"Is this what is called 'amok' in English?" I asked. "*Ji haa*", said the officer. "If you try and stop him, he will kill you with whatever he can get his hands on." Then, after a brief pause, he said, "It's happened to each one of us some time or the other; and when it has, everybody has seized us and plunged us in water to cool us. Samiruddin is the only person it hasn't happened to, even once. Did you know him, Saheb? His body looked as if it was soft like an eel's, but feel him, and you'd discover he was as tough as the shell of the tortoise. The Chinese chef on board the ship weighed close to three maunds – Samiruddin could flatten him with one blow. His practice with his lathi had given his arms the might of the tiger's paw. But the fact that he didn't go *emokh* didn't have anything to do with his physical strength – it was because of his *himmat*, his mental strength. He had decided that he would earn, come what may, he would earn and he would earn; he had absolutely forbidden himself from catching a *bimaari,* convinced himself that he wouldn't faint."

The *Serang* went on, "With what great *taqlif* did we reach Kuloom city, sweating out our lives".

"Where's that?" I asked.

"What is called Lanka in Bangla," he replied.

"Oh! You mean Colombo", I said.

"*Ji.* Our pronunciation isn't as correct as yours. We say, Kuloom city. They let us get down to walk about on land, but those who had gone out for the first time were watched very closely lest they should try to escape the unbearable hardships of the ship. Samiruddin didn't even get down at the port. Getting down means unnecessary expenses, he said. And, right he was, too, *huzoor*. The amount of cash *khalasis* blow at ports – one who has never seen a five-rupee note in his life, never earned more than eight annas – fifteen rupees on his hands, imagine. He rushes to buy baby crows!"

"We ate to our heart's content whatever we wished to eat, particularly, green vegetables. What is so common on land is a rarity for *khalasis*. They hardly have it, if at all."

"Then, it was on to Adan port."

This time, I didn't have to pronounce it A-E-D-E-N, the English way.

"Then, it was across the Red Sea to Susor Canal – the desolate desert on both sides, sand and sand everywhere, and just a narrow strip of water in between."

I understood that 'Susor Canal' was actually the Suez Canal.

"Poursoi, then. That was at the end of the canal. What a port, terrific. We disembarked there to have fresh green vegetables; the more worldly-wise among us went off to disreputable places."

I saw that the officer chap was aware of the fame of the Port Said brothels.

"From Poursoi to Marsai, and from Marsai to Hambur – Hambur is in Germany".

By then, I had come to grips with how foreign words sound when pronounced in a Sylheti accent. So, I understood that he was talking of Marseilles and Hamburg. I also noticed that the officer had picked up the names from people speaking in French and German; he pronounced them the way they spoke, not the derived English way.

"All the cargo was downloaded at Hambur," said the Serang. "Then we loaded her up again and crossed the sea to reach Nyuk (New York) port in Mirikin land."

"Whether you're a fresher or an old hand, it's the same here;

nobody is allowed to disembark at Nyuk port. Things are very strict there, and why shouldn't they be? Mirikin *mulk* is the land of gold; ordinary people like us can earn five-seven hundred a month there. People even darker than us, absolutely jet-black men, earn more than that there. If the *khalasis* are allowed to get down, they would all run away and spread across the entire *mulk* and earn money to their heart's content. That would apparently harm Mirikin workers no end. So, we stayed imprisoned in the ship."

"Samiruddin developed a complicated stomach problem three days before we reached Nyuk. The rest of us would often pretend to be sick and try to skip work, but Samiruddin had never played any such tricks and so the doctor instructed him to rest."

"The evening we reached Nyuk, Samiruddin called me, swore me to secrecy and told me that he would jump ship. Then he explained to me carefully how he planned to reach the shore."

"You won't believe me, Saheb, when I tell you of the detailed plans and well thought-out arrangements he had designed. From Calcutta's Chorabazaar (the stolen-goods market), he had bought a fine blue suit, shirt, tie collar, shoes and socks."

"The only thing I could do was to get him a brass pan. Camouflaged by the twilight, Samiruddin went down to the sea in his swimming shorts from the wrong end of the ship, i.e., towards the open sea. The pan had his suit, shoes, socks and one towel. He will take a circuitous route and will push the pan with his chest as he swims towards the coast half-a-mile away. On reaching land, he will dry himself with the towel, throw the shorts and the pan into the sea and, go off whistling towards the city. He had already sent a message to a Sylheti there from Hambur. He will go underground there for a few days until the police stop searching for him. Then, he will shave his moustache and his beard and will go far away from Nyuk to where the Sylheti community mint hard cash. It wasn't as if there was no risk of falling into the police's dragnet while attempting to jump ship, but once he managed to get on the road in his suit, the police would easily mistake him for a Nyuk native who had come to the shore to get some fresh air."

"The *pe-lan* came off all right, Saheb. There was a hunt for Samiruddin the next afternoon. By that time, not only had the bird flown the nest, he had totally vanished into the forest. Absolutely without a trace. A bird may even be found in the forest, but which police source has the ability to find Samiruddin in Nyuk City?"

Taking a break from the story-telling, the officer went to say the mid-day *namaaz*. When he returned, he said without making any kind of run-up, "After that, huzoor, I spent seven whole years on ships. I have landed at Kidderpore a few times, but I didn't have the *fursat* to make it home to my land. And, why would I go, anyway? My parents were dead, I didn't have a wife either. I used to send my old man money as long as he was alive. The old man spent his last few years happily – in Khuda's name – the old woman apparently used to cry for me. What will a few drops of salt water back home do to a man whom the endless brine of the sea hasn't been able to affect, huzoor?"

It made sense, whatever he said, but a drop of salty water appeared in his eyes too.

"Anyway," said the officer, "these seven years, I've had news – call it rumours if you will – from somebody or the other. Samuriddin has earned a lot of money – he is said to send money back home as well, but he has set up home in the Mirikin *mulk,* and doesn't seem to have any intention of returning home. I didn't rue the fact because who knows where Allah chooses a man to prosper."

"Then, I slipped on oil in the machine room and broke my leg. I stopped working for the big ships and returned home to work in the dispatch department. A couple of days after I came to this ship, I was going to say the *namaaz* early one morning when I was startled to see Samiruddin sitting on the deck. I hugged him to my breast. Brother, Samiruddin. In an instant, memories of my brotherly love for Samiruddin came rushing in."

"But, I was even more surprised to see that he didn't respond to any of my overtures. He kept sitting like a lifeless statue facing the water. "I didn't get the news of your home-coming?"

I asked. "Now, where are you travelling on this ship? Calcutta? Why? Didn't you like it at home?"

"He doesn't say a word. He kept sitting like a fakir and looking the other way as if he hadn't seen me at all."

"I realised something was wrong. Rather than try and get him to talk right then, I pushed and pulled him to my cabin. I held before him the breakfast plate, loaded with fried eggs and parathas. This used to be his favourite – now, he doesn't want to taste anything. Still, I forced something down his throat just as men force-feed a bereaved mother. Huzoor, you can do many things for somebody else, you can even sacrifice your life to save him, but how can you eat for somebody else?"

"That afternoon, I refused to let him land at Goaland. Huzoor, I remembered what had happened so many years back, when we were prevented from landing at Nyuk port, that was when Samiruddin had done his disappearing trick."

"Samiruddin finally began to open up in the darkness of night."

"He began to say, of his own accord, what had happened."

Serang was silent for some time. Was it because he wanted to rest his lungs, or was there some other reason, I didn't understand. I didn't prod him, either. "How do I tell you faithfully his sad tale, Saheb? I still remember – he told me everything in the inky darkness of the cabin. Each of his words had drilled a hole in the darkness and had struck my ears and, he had told the whole story in few words."

"During those seven years, he had sent almost twenty thousand rupees home to his younger brother. Twenty-thousand rupees – I don't know how much that is; I've never seen that much money together."

"Neither do I, I haven't seen it either," I replied.

"So, you understand, huzoor, how many lives you have to sacrifice to earn that money."

"When he sent the first five hundred rupees, he told his brother to pay the money-lender and redeem the mortgage on the house. The next thousand, thousand-five hundred was to buy the fallow land next door. Much, much more money, thereafter, to get a pond dug, then, more money still, for four large structures with walls of tiles, whitewashed the way they do it in the city. Then, there was the money for the agricultural land, the bullocks, the cows, the cow-shed, the granary, a pond for the women behind the house and, finally, there was the five thousand rupees for a brick-and-cement masjid this side of the pond, just opposite the *tongighar.*"

"Samiruddin had worked an inhuman two, two-and-a-half shifts a day in Mirikin *mulk* for seven years to earn his money. Every cowrie of his income is *halaal* income. Even a beggar in the Mirikin *mulk* wouldn't be able to survive on what he had spent on himself.

"He has funnelled back all his money to build the house and to buy land. So that he can return home and live the way the Mirikins do – build farms and live in fashionable houses like gentlemen."

"The brother, at the other end, had been briefing him regularly about the progress of the work. When he read that the masjid was ready, he headed for home. Even a black novice can get a job without difficulty on a ship at Nyuk port. And Samiruddin had learnt how to handle the machines so well, thanks to his work experience at various factories, he had a nice job on his way back to Kidderpore. He alighted from the ship in the evening and went straight to Sealdah. He spent the night on the platform and boarded the Chittagong Mail early next morning. He reached Srimangal Station at three a.m. From there, he started out for Dhalaichhora; it's eight miles away, and he would reach home by daybreak."

"Beyond the road comes a quarter-of-a-mile of paddy fields; then one reaches Dhalaichhora village."

"Samiruddin reached the paddy field with the first rays of the sun."

"The masjid was supposed to have a high turret, because the design for the masjid had been made for Samiruddin by an Egyptian engineer, and huzoor, too, has spent a long time in Egypt; he has seen the splendour of Egyptian turrets more than we have."

"The turret can be seen from so far away, that, you know, I, too, know, and so did Samiruddin."

"Samiruddin was surprised he couldn't see the turret. Then,

he advanced gradually – where was the pond, where, the tiled tower-house?"

"How come?" I asked in wonder.

It was as if the *Serang* hadn't heard my question at all. He went on, as if in a trance. "Nothing. The old broken-down thatched hut had become even older. When he left home, the house had stood on four bamboo poles; today, he sees there are six. Has the brother, then, built the houses in some other part of the village? But, then, he would have surely told him so in one of his letters. He suddenly comes across Basit Mullah from their village. Mullahji loves all of us a lot. He gave Samiruddin a tight, warm hug."

"At first, he, too, was reluctant to say anything. Later, under pressure from Samiruddin, he told him the truth, standing in the middle of the paddy field. His brother had puffed away all the money. Initially at Srimangal, Kulauda and Maulvibazaar, and later in Calcutta – on horses, women and what not."

Unable to restrain myself any longer, I said, "What's that you say, Serang? Can a man stand such a blow? But, how come nobody from the village wrote to him about it?"

"How could they know what Samiruddin was sending the money for?" asked the officer. The elder brother earns in lakhs abroad, Samiruddin's brother told them. He sends me some of it so that I can enjoy myself. Nobody had read Samiruddin's letters; he didn't have to get his letters read by anyone. Like me, Samiruddin is illiterate, but he had sent that bastard of a brother to the *paathshala* to be educated. Still, after seeing him blowing so much money, Mullahji and some others from the village had advised him to invest in a house and to buy land. He had reportedly answered, "My elder brother hasn't married; he has settled down in Mirkin *mulk* and won't return to this country again. And, even if he does, he'll bring back a lakh of rupees and will build ten houses in the space of three days."

"What a mean person!" I said. "Then?"

The *Serang* said, "Samiruddin didn't enter the village. He went back to Srimangal Station from the paddy field. Samiruddin didn't tell me, but I know Mullahji must have tried to persuade him to go to his house. In any case, he didn't turn back. He had only said he was going back where he had come from. The train to Calcutta leaves at eight p.m. Mullahji and the leaders of the village had brought the brother to the station – he was in the village that day as he had run out of money. He wrapped his arms round Samiruddin's legs, asked for his forgiveness and tried to convince him to return home. The others, too, said, "Come home. You can always go to Mirkin later on if you want to, but you've returned after so many years; rest a couple of days before you leave."

"With what face did the rascal come to his brother?" I asked.

"That's what I wonder, too. But, you know what Samiruddin did? He didn't kick his brother – nothing – only said he wouldn't go back home."

"Early next morning, I met him on this ship. I have already told you, he was as quiet as the statue at Shah port."

With a fresh breath of air, the *Serang* said, "Samiruddin told me everything in just a few words. But, huzoor, I couldn't understand what he murmured to himself at the end of the conversation. I remember the words, though. The beggar dreams he has become rich, he had said. When he wakes up, he finds things haven't changed at all. I had become a rich man by sending money back home to build a house, he had sighed. Where am I left now that that world has broken down?"

If this had been a story, a dream, and not a true story, then we could have ended here. But, as I am writing down whatever I heard, it will be an injustice if I don't tell the rest of *Serang*'s story.

"Fourteen years have passed since then," said *Serang*, "but I always have the feeling that Samiruddin bled his heart out in the darkness of my cabin yesterday evening.

"But, that *insaaf* you talked about, huzoor – remember? – who will take care of that?

"Samiruddin returned to Mirikin *mulk* and made another thirty thousand in ten years. This time, he didn't send his brother any money. He died in the ship on his way back home with the money. Since he had nobody else in this wide world, the money made its way to the same brother. Again, he blew the money."

"*Insaaf* – where?"

(originally published in Bangla as *Nonajal)*

DACOIT MOTHER

Satinath Bhaduri

Translated By Sayantan Dasgupta

Earlier, she was the Dacoit Wife. After Saukhi's dad died, people knew her as Dacoit Mother. Will it do if Dacoit Mother's sleep is not light? There is no saying when, in the middle of the night, there'll be a knock on the door. A series of three, double tock-tocks would mean that somebody from the band had come with money. A fourth tock-tock would mean Saukhi himself has returned home. The son, you know, has issued a strict order – Don't open the door in a huff. Careful! Wait for as long as it takes to breathe in and out ten times. Then, open the door. There are so many other tock-tock codes. They've been devised so many times, changed so many times. Whom will you trust in this world? You can deal with the police, but, when a member of the band begins to get ideas, it becomes really tough to deal with him. Times have really changed. She'd heard tales about those days from Saukhi; somebody from the band had cut off his own tongue after he'd been wounded and captured lest he should spill the beans to the police. And, today ... Saukhi has been in jail these five years. The first two years, the members of the band used to reach them money regularly. From the third year, all that stopped. Could anything like this have happened in the past? Justice, duty – have all these things simply vanished from the earth? How many times has Saukhi's old man gone to jail, Saukhi himself has been incarcerated twice earlier; the band has never behaved like this before. The money would reach them even before the month got over – in advance sometimes, three or four months in one go. But, look at things this time. The band didn't even glance at them to see if the family was washed away by poverty. The first wife had a strong body. Saukhi's present wife is lean and sickly. And, after she delivered her son, her health has really broken down. When Saukhi got caught this time, the wife was with child. Come to think of it, yes, the grandson is four-five years old. What misfortune he has been born into. He whose old man's name makes the chowkidar shudder – even the Darogasaheb hasn't dared to ever address his father except in the respectable form – he doesn't get two square meals a day, what a thing to happen! And this wife, with her poor health, cannot do hard work. I am an old woman, I go from door to door, selling *khoi-muri.* It's difficult to even satisfy my own hunger with what comes from it, it was not for nothing that *bouma* had to be sent to her father's house. Besides, she's from a milkman's family; we can't go around doing menial work in people's houses. Who would let us, anyway; would anyone trust Saukhi's wife and mother? If I had a choice, wouldn't I like to live with my daughter-in-law and grandson? *Beaii* has two buffaloes; at least the woman and the child are getting a few drops of milk. They need the milk. Saukhi will be free in just another year or so. Then he'll bring his wife back and cover her with silver. We'll show the neighbours that Saukhi's mother's grandson is not a street beggar. Just let Saukhi come back. These humbugs in the band will have to be dealt with, too. I say, what is the need to have these selfish men into the band. They're not worth being called 'dacoits'; thieves, petty thieves – that's what they are. The one who used to come with the money – have you taken a look at him? Thin as a reed. A wisp of a beard below the chin. Paint your face, wield the *mashaal* in your hand – whatever you do – will anyone ever be scared by a man so thin and unimpressive?

Sleep evades her. It's the same story every night. Come winter, and she can never sleep unless she tucks herself all the way up to the head inside the quilt. Once, Saukhi had come back from somewhere in the dead of the night, and his tock-tocks had not elicited any response. How he had thrashed his mother then. He had declared – next time I find you sleeping with your face tucked inside the quilt, I'll kill you straightaway. He's his father's son, no wonder he has such a temper. These last five years, there has been nobody to say so much as a word even if she covered every inch of her body and snored her way to Kingdom Come. No mean sorrow, this.

In spite of her problems going to sleep, she has not slept with her face tucked inside the quilt even once these last five years. All because of her son.

Outside, there was a rustle on the dry fallen leaves, near the trunks of the nona-aata trees. Perhaps, *gondhogokul*, or maybe a fox or something like that. Who knows what morsels they come in search of. The cold has become more fierce as she has aged. Earlier, how well the solitary quilt used to do! This quilt has become pretty old, too. The last time, Saukhi had brought it from jail. That wasn't exactly yesterday!

She has to stop midway through her calculations about the age of the quilt. The tock-tock sound of a knock seemed to reach her ears. Perhaps, the clucking of a lizard. When the elephant is in trouble, even the frog kicks him! Even the lizard has started teasing her to get some fun. Let it!

Tock-tock! Another two knocks sounded on the door.

No! It's not a lizard. Its a metallic sound – the sound of tapping on the tin door.

The old woman sat up. She had lit a fire on the floor to warm the house; it has gone out, who knows when. But the smoke has made the darkness in the room even more dense. So, the idiots of the band have remembered Saukhi's mother after all these days.

Another two taps sounded on the door. No more doubt. After so many days out of the game, this little incident has brought a spark of excitement into the old woman's life. Still, you never know – who knows who it is –

Saukhi's mother gets up slowly and goes and stands by the door. She tries to see the man outside through the slit at the edge of the closed door. The man, too, it seems, is trying to peer inside through the slit. It's pitch black outside as well; not a single thing can be seen. The smell of beedi drifts to her nose. Another tock-tock! Almost in her ear, this time. Strange – this tap wasn't supposed to be there! Then, the man is not here to give her money; it's not somebody from the police, is it? Maybe he doesn't know the secret code of the taps properly. There's still a long way to go before Saukhi gets free. This must be the police. Doesn't matter who you are, though, I'll definitely accept money if you offer me – the consequences, we can think about later. I'll have to speak cautiously. I mustn't carelessly blurt out details about the band and its members.

She suddenly remembers she's supposed to wait for ten counts before she opened the door. She's so excited she can hardly breathe, how is she supposed to count? Her heart is pounding. The old woman rapidly goes through the motions of breathing in and out ten times, just for tradition's sake.

Who's that?

She opens the door and seeing the tall, well-built man in front of her, even a Dacoit Mother feels a shiver down her spine.

"I say, the house is pitch dark. How do I see where I'm going?"

"Who? Saukhi? It's you?! I had no idea it was you ..."

The old woman has the son in her embrace. This boy has grown old, but he hasn't changed a bit. He's been released from jail; he could easily have made a spectacle and come home with his head held high, waking up the neighbours. But no, he had to tap on the door furtively and play games with his mother! Where can she hide her joy?

"The *Laatsaheb* had gone to see the jail. He was impressed with my work and ordered my release. His whim, you know. I had bribed the head sweeper; he'd recommended me to the jailer babu. That was how I got an extra remission. *Acchha*, you light the *kupi* first, then we'll see about the rest."

Saukhi uttered the words louder than he needed to, so that the others in the house could hear him as well. Then, he struck a match and held it up to help his mother look for the kerosene vessel.

Only now did the old woman see her son's face. There's quite a bit of grey in his hair. That is why the son's face has begun to look like a reflection of his father's. Looks a bit thin, doesn't he? But Saukhi's health always improves whenever he goes to jail – just like his old man. Then, why is it this way this time? Her son's eyes scan the room all the way up to the furthest wall, as if, looking for something. The old woman doesn't have to be told who he is looking for.

"Tell me, child, you didn't fall ill in jail, did you?"

Saukhi doesn't want to negotiate that question. He asks, "I don't see any of the others."

This is the question the old woman had been fearing all this while. He was sure to ask, still –

"*Bou* has gone to her father's place."

"Why, all of a sudden?"

He's come back home after such a long time; she doesn't want to tell him everything and spoil his mood so soon. A grown-up man's anger! Who knows, he might run off immediately upon hearing the story, to go and settle things with the band! The daughter-in-law's and the grandson's illness – that, too, can wait. Saukhi, she knows, goes gaga over his son. The first wife didn't have any issue at all. This is the only one this wife has produced. Once he hears of his son's illness, Saukhi may leave this place at once. He's come after so many days – won't I be able to keep him close to me even for one day? Let him eat and rest for a day or two; then he can be told everything one by one.

"Why, can't a woman want to see her parents once in a while?"

"No, no, that's not what I'm saying ..." Saukhi is more disappointed than embarrassed. The happiness of his homecoming has been halved in a moment. How many times has he tried to imagine what his son looks like! How long he had stayed with his ear against the door before he'd knocked, trying to hear how his son prattles with his mother! Surely, nine was too early for the mischievous boy to go off to sleep. He fixes things up in his mind – he'll go to his in-laws tomorrow itself to bring his wife and son back. It doesn't seem a good idea to tell Ma about his plan right now. She will think that the new wife has taken her son away from her. Ma is saying so many things; it is only now that he hears her final words.

"Come, go and have a wash."

"No, no, I've already eaten. Don't you sit down to cook in this middle of the night."

"Who's cooking? There's some *khoi-muri*. Finish it off. Don't I know whether you've eaten or not."

When he was about to go to bed after finishing off the *khoi-muri,* that was tomorrow's merchandise, he suddenly noticed the torn quilt on Ma.

"Give that to me."

Overriding her protests, Saukhi drapes his own quilt over Ma's body. Even then, coccooned in the new quilt, the old woman cannot go to sleep. Her feet refused to thaw. All kinds of worries have got her disturbed. The sound of Saukhi's regular snores echo in her ears. The boy has come home after so many days; the mother should be happy and at peace with herself, but no. What would she feed him the next morning – that is what is bothering her. Tonight, the *khoi-muri* merchandise did the trick. If he'd said he felt like having some rice, then, that would have been it. She would have had no other option but to tell him everything. How Saukhi loves having *alur charchari*. He probably hasn't been able to have it for such a long time in jail. Potatoes, rice, mustard oil – everything has to be bought – where will I get so much money from? How can she tell her son, first thing in the morning – go, get some money, then I'll cook you something.

The clock struck two in the kutcheri. There is no solution in sight. She remembered that masons were at work in Peshkarsaheb's house. When she'd gone there to sell *muri* today, she'd seen that the fallen northern wall was being re-constructed. The old woman got up from the bed and shuffled quietly out of the room.

Matadeen Peshkar's house is not too far. The wall had been raised to a height of two arm-lengths, or, maybe two and a half. The old woman didn't have much trouble climbing over the wall, thanks to the heap of earth and broken bricks lying around. The house seemed dead.

It's difficult to discern in the dark what lies where. Peshkarsaheb's khadams and his *ghoti* (which served as his *lota*) filled with water have been kept carefully near the door to the verandah. He'll need them first thing in the morning. The old woman was so scared that she didn't try to grope her way through the courtyard to find out what else was lying about there. She picked up the *ghoti*, climbed over the wall and came out quietly. Not a drop of the water spilled out from it. So late into the night, nobody would suspect anything even if they saw her with the *lota* in hand.

In this land, life comes to a standstill without the *lota*. Matadeen Peshkar's fingers begin to itch if he doesn't hold the *lota* in his hands a couple of times. Thus, there was a major commotion in his house in the morning.

Khoka's Ma set up a nasal wail and reminded her husband that the *lota* is the Lakshmi of the house; a new one must be bought immediately in order to ensure the prosperity of the family. The master's belching smoke from his nostrils, he is so angry with the thief. "Don't talk crap! That's all you fellows can do. It's clearly written in the law – if a theft is reported to the police, the thief can even be sent to jail." Legal-smart Matadeen left the house to report the incident to the thana, making many other jagged comments to Khoka's Ma.

On his way back, he dropped in at the utensils shop. The shopkeeper showed him many different types of *ghotis*, but there was nothing that impressed Matadeen. Peshkarsaheb is very fussy when it comes to *lotas*. He wants a *ghoti* with a raised base ... see – such a big one – it must have a wide mouth so that a well-built woman's hand, *kankan* and all, could easily slip into it to rinse it clean. The shopkeeper finally gives up and asks, will an old one do? Old in name only, you'll get it cheap, just two-and-a-half rupees.

"Oh, used utensils are sold here, too, are they? Let's have a look."

One look at the *ghoti* and he knew something was wrong.

He took out his glasses from his pocket and placed them on the bridge of his nose – that star etched just there, on the base. No question about it ...

Forgetting the writs of law, Matadeen peshkar seizes the shopkeeper's throat. "Come on, spit it out, where did you get this *lota*? You sit in your shop in the daytime, and burgle homes at night! There was such a hue and cry! People crowded around the shop. The shopkeeper says that he has counted out fourteen anna paisas and bought his *ghoti* from Saukhi's mother – only a little while ago."

"This *ghoti* can be got for fourteen annas, you mean? You bought it, knowing full well that it was stolen. You know the writ for harbouring stolen goods?"

Peshkarsaheb sent a young lad to the *thana* to get the *daroga*. There's no laxity in Darogasaheb's discharge of his duties once the thief has been caught. He arrived immediately on his cycle. After he'd heard everything, he cycled all the way to Saukhi's house with his force. Saukhi's mother is preparing potato curry on the *unoon*. Her son is yet to leave the comfort of the bed. He's had to get up dot by the watch in jail for a long time; Saukhi has told himself that he will celebrate his new-found freedom by not getting up before noon – come what may, he won't.

Seeing the daroga and the policemen, the old woman's heart skips a beat. She's not the person to panic on seeing the police; she has seen the police charge into their house so many times at such ungodly hours before this! But things are so different today. Matadeen peshkar and the shopkeeper are with the police. She'd had the idea that shopkeepers did not sell old utensils without touching them up and giving them a new look. The police had gheraoed their house once five, or maybe seven years ago, in search of guns. Why, her head hadn't drooped then. Dacoity is her husband's and her son's profession by right. That's a man's job, a job that carries a lot of pride. Having to go to jail is simply a matter of bad luck, nothing more than that. But this is theft. Petty theft, that's what it is.

Saukhi's mother has forgotten to even deny the allegations, so ashamed is she.

Darogasaheb asks her, "Did you sell this *lota* to the utensils shop in the bazaar for fourteen annas?"

Not a word came out of the old woman's lips. She only looked at her son once and bent her head.

Saukhi finally gets it. Ma has ended up stealing a *ghoti* for the sake of fourteen annas. Why didn't Ma tell him? His duty had been in the godown of the jailhouse. He has earned ninety rupees from the jail contractors. Even now, that money is in the batua at his waist. Why didn't Ma ask him for it? What else do you expect from a woman? Maybe one look at the house should have told him enough to understand the precarious condition of the household – he should have understood and given his mother the money of his own accord. But when did he get the time? He'd reached home at night and gone to bed, and he hadn't got up till now. Of all things, stealing a *lota*? While he was in jail, he had never even spoken to the petty thieves. In jail, lifers are the ones dacoits chat up with – this is not unknown to Ma. Petty thieves are only sentenced to two or three months – doesn't Ma know?

"Aeei, you old hag! Why don't you answer my question? Come on, out with it!"

The old woman is silent. One can't even understand from her face if Darogababu's question has got through to her.

Saukhi couldn't hold himself back any longer.

"Darogasaheb, why involve women? I stole the *ghoti* last night."

The all-knowing Darogababu flashed a triumphant smile at his underlings and tried to convince them that he had realized this as soon as he had seen Saukhi sleeping so late; he was only trying to get the words out of the old hag's mouth.

At this point, Saukhi's mother broke down. She has brought shame to his son's name.

"No, no, Darogasaheb! Saukhi didn't do it; I did. Let him go, Darogasaheb. He hasn't even met his wife and his son yet –

The old woman throws herself at Darogababu's feet. But he doesn't want to tax himself with the shopkeeper or the old hag; his business is with the real culprit.

When he was about to leave, Saukhi fished the botua from his waist and left it on the *khatia*.

Ma was still lying on the ground, sobbing her heart out. The smell of burnt potato curry emanates from the *unoon* and spreads across the entire neighbourhood.

(Originally published in Bangla as *Dakat-er Ma*)

THE ARTISTE

Manik Bandyopadhyay

Translated By Suchorita Chattopadhyay

Madan was sitting in the courtyard soaking in the winter morning sun when he suddenly developed a terrible cramp in his leg.

Not having spun his loom for a whole week at a stretch, he had developed a stiffness, a kind of numbing, rheumatic pain in his limbs, waist and back. On top of that there was a shooting pain in the joints. Thread is in short supply, the loom does not run, it really gets one down; like being ill without any disease. Working on the loom means the same monotonous movement hour after hour. Its absence weakens the body, makes one drowsy and lethargic within a couple of days. One cannot sleep. The heart bleeds with a suffering that borders on ennui, as if everything has come to an end. It is the way one feels when one goes to a *jatra* and sees Nimai renouncing the world and walking off, a *sanyasi* – only here the agony is stronger and apparently never ending. Madan endures the worries of the body and the mind and remains silent. Why won't he endure what can be endured.

Ma has gone to the master's house early in the morning and she has taken her daughter-in-law (Madan's wife), along with her They have gone to plead with the womenfolk of the family and to try and get an order for weaving a few exquisite sarees woven by Madan, the reputed weaver, on the occasion of the wedding of their younger daughter,

If they can get an order from the master's family, they would probably be able to procure the thread easily enough. The master's name counts after all. Madan's *Mashi* is the only other person in the house. One of her hands is maimed and she is thin as a reed. On hearing Madan's screams of pain she comes running, carrying Madan's two-year-old son. With them comes *Mashi's* four-year-old daughter. How could *Mashi* possibly yank his cramped leg straight with her one hand. *Mashi* also starts screaming. Scared by Madan's cries, the two children had already started crying at the top of their voices.

At that point Bhuban Ghosal comes in from the street, and immediately understanding what needs to be done, he grabs Madan's ankle and gives a few sudden tugs and slaps hard on his thighs. As the pain becomes tolerable, Madan slowly regains control over his leg; instead of writhing and collapsing he begins to regain his composure. "Thank God you were around. I don't know what would have happened otherwise."

Sucking in his cheeks and taking a series of deep breaths, Madan rubs his hands on his legs. The friction of the rough calloused palms on the dry cracked skin of the legs makes a sound similar to the one he makes with his mouth.

"Get up and try walking." Bhuban advises him, "you'll recover."

Madan doesn't say anything. Hearing the commotion, a number of men and women from the nearby houses have come running. Udi is the only one who has not come from her adjoining hut. Only a few banana trees separate Madan's hut from Udi's. She is screaming in her sickly-sweet voice that irritates the entire weaver colony – "What happened? Tell me what has happened?"

Bhuban has apparently come by the road, but everybody knows that he has actually come from Udi's hut – he has taken the road after circling the pond. Probably Udi herself has sent him here in a hurry. Madan's loom has not been running for the last seven days and his wife is nine months pregnant. From yesterday Udi has been worrying in case someone dies of starvation in her house. She had called Madan's wife aside and had given her some rice and *daal.* Quietly she has asked about Madan's moods, she has tried to find out whether Madan has finally changed his mind and agreed to weave ordinary sarees against a fixed charge like all the others. But Madan's wife had wept and told Udi – no, Madan is still adamant.

The sight of Bhuban here visibly changes the expressions of the people who have come running from the nearby houses. Meanwhile *Pishi* has given Bhuban a *pidi,* a low stool, to sit on. Everybody keeps staring at Madan and Bhuban with curiosity writ large in their eyes. Has he too finally given in to Bhuban? Is he finally agreeing to weave cheap dhoti, sarees and *gamchhas* at merely a slave's wage!

Madan feels uneasy. He rubs the unshaven stubble on his face with the palm of his hand.

Almost in reply to the unspoken questions of the people around him, Madan addresses Old Bhola and says, "I had developed a sudden cramp in my leg. O God! It was so painful – it was deadly. I was almost dying when he came running and yanked my leg and set it right. He saved me."

The short and plump wife of Gagan weaver utters a peculiar sound and says, "Oh! He must have been somewhere quite near and could come here fast – that's what we were all wondering."

"I don't feel too well because I have not been running the loom," Madan says quickly. He is terribly scared of Gagan's wife's tongue.

Brindaban is standing in the background like a culprit. His hut too adjoins Madan's dwelling, across a mango tree to the north; the branches of the tree almost touch the thatched roofs of both the huts.

Brindaban is much younger than old Bhola but his health

has broken down far more. He has only an old dilapidated loom – *gamchhas* and eight arm-length long sarees are all that can be woven on it. He does not sit at the loom any more; he just doesn't have the strength. His eldest son Rasik runs the loom. The shortage of thread has forced all the looms in the weavers' colony to close down, scarcity and fear haunt the entire weaver colony. The only looms that are running belong to Keshab and Brindaban.

Bhuban asks Brindaban innocently, "How many *gamchhas* have been woven Brindaban?" Brindaban is startled and takes a step backwards.

"I don't know sir, my son would know."

"Ask Keshab to collect the money after he finishes weaving."

Brindaban tries once to straighten his bent back and gives everybody a helpless pathetic look.

"Please ask my son sir. I know nothing about it."

Brindaban turns and walks away slowly.

Gagan's wife makes a face and snaps, " I know nothing sir, my son knows what tricks the old man knows!"

Old Bhola says, "Oh! Why don't you shut up, Buno's *ma!* Why waste your words? Madan, is your pain better? Then let us go."

Keshab will get the money as soon as he goes. It is possible to get money if you can only weave *gamchhas* and sarees – such words, such ideas scare them. There is no earning in any of the houses, only starvation.

Bhuban says, "You know Madan, the weavers in your village are all idiots."

Weaving has been Madan's family tradition for generations. In a fit of anger he turns sarcastic. "Of course! Weavers are a race of fools."

Bhuban goes on with what he has to say. "You are not getting thread, eh ! You won't get it for sometime either. What's the point in keeping your loom idle? Mihirbabu is offering you thread, go ahead with your weaving and whatever you get will be your profit. Instead you decide not to weave at all if you are not allowed to buy thread. What nonsense is this? Your point, at least, I understand, you are not ready to weave cheap sarees, but what about them?"

"It doesn't suit them. Everybody doesn't buy thread nor can everybody. You know most of them run their looms on borrowed money. They run the loom day and night to make ends meet, working themselves to death. You want to halve even that, how can we accept that?"

"Otherwise we don't make any profit, dear. Do you have any idea how much we have to spend on thread?" Bhuban lets out a deep sigh of regret and says, "Anyway, what can I do. I pleaded so hard with the master and got him to allot some thread to you. Now, if you say no, what can be done? I understand your problem, but times are not good, so hold on to your loom and somehow make ends meet. Otherwise, you may soon have to sell off your looms."

"When times change and thread becomes available, you'll remember this Bhuban Ghosal – keep this in mind – you'll regret it then – if only you had listened to me, your loom would have been safe and you would also have survived."

If the loom is pawned or sold, Bhuban himself will buy it on Mihirbabu's behalf. Probably the man is sitting tight, based on that conviction. But will things go that far? Who knows, the weavers may take thread from Bhuban and start weaving even before that.

Mashi comes and starts fidgeting. A Brahmin's son has touched Madan's feet – so *Mashi* can't rest in peace till Madan prostrates himself at Bhuban's feet. It hasn't occurred to Madan it seems, or may be he has forgotten. When Madan stretches his legs towards Bhuban's feet, *Mashi* finally loses her patience. She whispers into Madan's ears and reminds him about touching Bhuban's feet.

Madan gets extremely irritated; he doesn't pick up the girl. She goes on crying, "Get lost, I don't even want to see your face."

Mashi with the children in tow. She is familiar with Madan' fit of temper. Scolding the daughter for crying is just an excuse. Why people should get upset if children scream into their ears, is something *Mashi* doesn't know, and Madan doesn't understand either. The cries of the children do not reach Madan's ears. They are like the incessant clatter of the loom, the chatter of women and the call of the crickets. Madan's temper has soured. So what if he hasn't touched the feet of the Brahmin's son? *Mashima's* faith in Madan is staunch. He sings *Ramayana* to tune, he has kept up his father's reputation in weaving, Madan weaver gets orders for making the best goods. When *Mashi* first came to this house at the time of the master's forefathers, Madan's father had teased her by weaving a saree as flimsy as net for her to wear. *Mashi* will never forget those days. Today times are bad, orders don't come, thread is not available, the looms do not run but even so, Madan does not weave cheap sarees. *Mashi* feels bad for him as she thinks about his father. His mother and wife behave somewhat strangely with him.

Mashi thinks, if only Madan's father had been alive today. Had he been alive, his age would have been more than four scores and a half, *Mashi* does not understand that very well. She only feels very depressed to think that he would have been older than Sridhar. Looking at Sridhar's misfortune, still alive in this condition, she herself prays for the old man's death.

It doesn't matter if Madan's father is no more. Madan at least is here.

Madan's *Ma* and wife come back slowly. Madan's wife, weighed down by her pregnancy, walks with heavy steps; for the last few days her limbs have been swollen. The tattered old saree she wears was woven for her by Madan himself at the time of their wedding. Even now, the exquisite border, the soft sheen of the fine weave – everything taken together – is still so beautiful that even if she were to wrap it around carelessly, she could well be taken for a woman from a well-off family, but for her matted unkempt hair and chapped flaky skin.

Madan's mother mutters to herself as she walks this way, bent double over her walking stick. Madan would have been happier if she had not said anything in front of Bhuban. But the old woman has no sense left. She comes near them and immediately starts off on how the womenfolk at the master's house had laughed and sniggered at them and had driven them away on hearing them soliciting orders for exquisite sarees that would guard the married women against misfortune. Are such sarees still in vogue? Grandmothers, maid-servants and peasant women are probably the only ones who wear such sarees these days.

Madan the weaver! Sarees woven by Madan the weaver! The fox who is the king in the bamboo grove!

They said this! They said so! Madan draws up his legs and sits up straight, too big for their boots, the masters have become too swollen headed. The masters have gone too far – pride comes before a fall.

Climbing onto the veranda , Madan's wife almost loses her balance. Clutching the post she somehow regains her balance and goes inside; her acrid comments come from within "He is not worth a single paisa, yet what pride!"

Bhuban consoles Madan and says, "Women talk like that

Madan, one shouldn't pay any heed to such words."

That they do, the womenfolk at the master's house talk like that, his mother and wife do so too and, so does Udi. But not all women talk like that. Many women, in this weaver colony itself, never talk like that. In fact they make Madan stand in the middle and fight with the men-folk of their family. Madan runs a loom, they also weave on looms, yet they are not worth the dust on Madan's feet. Madan raises a broken toothed smile amidst finger-length beard and moustache and says this to Bhuban. Such strength and tenacity from a rather insignificant weaver strikes Bhuban as a bit odd. There is also a touch of anger and a certain envy gnawing at his insides. Recently, after getting involved in Mihirbabu's weaving business, he had heard that there was a common saying among the weaving community of this area, "The day Madan weaves a *gamchha* ..." Initially he had not understood the meaning of the saying properly; later he realized, the weavers of this area use these words instead of saying, "When the sun rises in the west." He knows that the day Madan agrees to take thread from him and weave sarees, the very next day most people from the weaver colony will come running to him to procure thread. The man is rather adamant and whimsical too; one moment he is sighing away to Kingdom come, the other he talks big as if he were some *Raja-Maharaja*.

As he is about to get up, Bhuban thinks he hears a moan from within the house.

Immediately there was *Mashi's cry.* "O Madan, quick, come and see what's wrong with your wife."

Bhuban goes and sends Udi back for news. It's late already, he should be going, he has a lot of work' But he can't leave till he gets the news from Madan's house. Madan may give in if that serious a misfortune befalls him. Waiting for Udi he gets irritated. That girl has the habit of getting too involved in everything having gone there to bring news she has probably ended up nursing Madan's wife. What has happened? If something serious happens ...

Udi comes back after a long time. Madan's wife had walked a long distance and was feeling unwell; she had even collapsed once. It seemed as if that was all there was, but now it seems that she will get her labour pains as well.

The woman will die if she has to deliver in this state. If she gets a fistful of rice at the time of one meal, she has to starve through the next three meals. It has been this way these last two months. I gave the man a piece of my mind. " Why don't you die?" I said.

She shoves in some wood and puts the vessel onto the fire again. Her indomitable spirit manifests itself in every movement of her short and tight body.. It is amazing that the earthen vessel doesn't crack when she dumps it into the fire.

"How come you've not gone as yet?"

"I'll go by and by. I am just feeling lazy."

"Do you want some rice? Rice cooked by me!" pleads Udi

Bhuban gets angry and says, " I don't like the way you talk."

Madan is sitting on the veranda. Bhuban peeps at him, circles around the pond and takes the road again. The *pidi* has been lying there since morning, he perches himself on it in royal style.

"How is your wife?"

"There's a bit of pain. There is more bleeding than pain. They've gone to get old Durga."

Madan's calm, unworried response unsettles Bhuban. He lights a *bidi* and begins to ponder; he offers Madan a *bidi too.*

Suddenly Madan says, "Why don't you let me weave something good, something expensive? Don't you have thread?"

Bhuban is filled with joy.

"I have some. But will you weave anything other than Benarasi?"

"Benarasi?" Madan says in a voice full of regret as if not weaving a Benarasi is his crime, his failure. "I've never woven a Benarasi in my life."

The thread arrives within the hour. Bhuban gets someone to reach the thread to Madan's house. The sight of the thread brings tears to his eyes. He will have to weave good cloth out of this thread! It would have been better if he had woven *gamchha* like Keshab. People would have said, "Circumstanccs have forced Madan the weaver to weave *gamchhas* but he has never woven cheap sarees." He feels a tightness somewhere in his chest, something like the cramp he had developed in his leg in the morning. The two rupees advance tucked away in his waist seems almost to singe his flesh. But not working the loom for so many days has produced a painful stiffness all over his body. The hunger dies and keeps waking up again and again and his wife keeps on moaning.

What should Madan the weaver do?

Late that night the village was sleeping in the dull haze of the winter moon, the surroundings were quiet and still. Only the occasional cries of dogs and foxes somewhere in the distance can be heard. A sound begins to emerge from the room which houses Madan's loom – thak a thak, thak a thak! Madan is weaving furiously on his loom and it is making a loud noise. The sound of the running loom reaches not just Udi's house, it wafts its way even to Brindaban's house.

Bhuban says, amazed, "He has started running the loom already? How did he manage to get everything ready all on his own?"

Udi is also amazed, "He's a genius, he can do everything." She says this and strains her ears in fear and amazement. Old Brindaban calls his son and asks him, "Is Madan running his loom?"

"What else?" Keshab replies sarcastically, "he's running the loom secretly in the middle of the night; it's wrong only if we do it."

"Maybe it is not Bhuban's thread!"

"Whose thread is it then? Tell me, who else has got thread?"

Udi does not know when Madan's loom stopped running. She gets up early in the morning and runs to Madan's house. She wakes Madan up and enthusiastically asks him, "How much did you weave?"

"Come and take a look."

Madan takes her to the weaving room. Udi is dumbstruck when she sees the empty loom. The bundle of thread lies there as before.

Madan gives the thread to Udi and also gives her the two rupees. He says, "Go and return it to Bhubanbabu. Tell him, the day Madan weaves a *gamchha* ..."

As the day progressed, half the men-folk and women of the weaver colony came in groups and stood in front of Madan's veranda. One look at their faces and it was clear what was going on in their minds. Tears of anger, tears of sorrow were welling up in the eyes of some of them. Even Gagan weaver's wife had fallen silent. Old Bhola asks, "Madan, is it true that you've taken thread from Bhuban, that you set up your loom secretly in the middle of the night

"Go and check."

"Didn't you run the loom at night?"

"Yes I did. An empty loom, My feet and hands were cramped from not having run the loom, that's why I ran the bare loom for a while. You think I will weave with Bhuban's thread? That

I'll betray you after giving you my word? The day Madan goes back on his word ..."

Suddenly Madan fell silent.

Originally published in Bangla as "*Shilpi.*"

SACRILEGE

Ashapurna Devi

Translated By Ipshita Chanda

Subhash-*Kakima's* name roused hisses of disgust on all sides. It seemed inconceivable that a woman-being could have such a hard heart.

Why only a woman-being, was it possible for any human being to be thus ? When an action that is impossible for man to perform is so easily performed by a woman, what will people stop at saying?

And can whatever they say be enough? My own *Kakima* and *Ma* came home and sat themselves down in the hall, legs stretched out , as if unable to withstand the jolt of this shock.

Subhash-*Kakima* is not related to us, so there are no hassles of *asauch*, the period of impurity. Besides – when married women come back from a house where death has occurred, it seems they shouldn't bathe immediately, so *Ma, Kakima* have only changed before sitting down. *Pishima*, though, came in only after a dip at the bathing-*ghat*.

Standing in the courtyard, wringing the edge of her widow's white borderless *thaan* garment, washing her feet with the droplets of water that she wrung, *Pishima* said, her voice sharp and clear, loud and direct. "That's it, then, at long last Girin Khuro's bag of bones are at rest. Aha, sorrows pursued him from birth. That skeletal frame, wracked by disease and grief, stuck on only because his life had not come to its divinely decreed end. Or else, he was as good as dead."

Taking down a coarse silk *thaan* from the clothes rack, she put it on, and then sitting next to *Ma*, she began to wipe her shaved head with its edge. *Ma* sighed and said, "Ever since I was born human, I haven't heard such a destructive thing, *Thakurjhi*."

"You were born the other day, *Bou*, your not having heard, is no great thing. Has anyone in the world ever heard the like?"

Kakima said, "I'm only thinking how could she? Didn't the life rip out of her? Not one day, not one and a half days, six or seven whole months! To suppress this awesome news and remain calm – oof! Unthinkable!"

"Heart made of stone!" said *Ma*.

Pishima said, "My dear, what is harboured within the heart is revealed only when the time comes. When that fellow Subhash was around, it seemed as if such great love was never seen on earth. And who can tell why that fellow pushed off – he must have sensed some other qualities inside his wife."

I know the fire of this criticism will not be easily extinguished. They will use all the possible terms to damn and shame, one by one. Only unfinished household chores might prod them to abandon their discussion.

After lying around quietly for a while in the middle of the day, I left the house, preoccupied.

Today is Sunday. I'm supposed to return to Calcutta by tonight's train. But I simply couldn't bring myself to leave. Perhaps the interminable discussions about Subash *Kakima* all day long have tired me out entirely.

Living an unruffled rural existence, these people make the most of the slightest event worthy of discussion, latching on to it for all it's worth. And this is such a terribly major event! Now – who knows what atonement ritual Subhash *Kakima* must undergo to return to purity. By the way, has Subhash *Kakima* committed some vile sin? Or has she infringed family duty, *Kuladharma*? Or has she broken social norms? What exactly she's done, it's rather difficult to say. But what she's done has probably never been done by anyone before, so there has been no discussion of *prayaschitt*, the atonement ritual, yet.

On the way back, I come upon a few people gathered upon Dinesh Roy's front porch, engaged in the same discussion. There are three or four almost extinguished lanterns with their wicks turned low parked on the steps leading upto the porch. It's too dark to recognise anyone exactly.

There's not much need to waste kerosene during *shuklapaksh*, the lunar quarter when the moon waxes – it's enough to tap your stick to announce your progress as you walk the paths at night. But things are different today. Today there's been a death in the village, so its good to have a touch of flame in your hand as you walk abroad once it's dark.

Village people's eyes glitter in the dark. As soon as he saw me, Dinesh Roy yelled out, "Who goes there? Is it Monotosh?"

I was forced to come forward.

Dinesh Roy said, "Why haven't you come out with a lantern on a day like this, *Babaji*?"

I replied, "I've been out since evening."

"Alright, sit a while. Surenda here will go past your gate, go together, he'll light up your way."

"I won't need that," so saying, I was ready to leave, but who'd let me go?

Dinesh Roy said loud and generous, "You may not need it, but I do. I can't let you go off alone in the dark. Come,come sit . So then – you're not returning tonight, are you?"

"No sir, I'll go tomorrow."

"D'you have a holiday tomorrow?"

"No, holiday for what?"

"So then?"

I know these people will not stop asking questions even when they see a clear reluctance on my part to answer. This is their uniqueness.

I said "Just didn't feel like going today."

Dinesh Roy gave a little high, false laugh and said, "Hhm! How can you feel like it, anyway? What you've seen and heard has left you completely wonderstruck, eh? You've heard of Subhash's wife's antics, haven't you?

"I have."

"You folk stay in Calcutta, I say, you must be used to seeing all kinds of new fangled stuff – have you seen anything like this there?"

I said very politely, "No sir."

Suren Sarkar cleared his throat. "You heard the excuse, of course? Has the gall to say, the old man would be totally shattered – so she did it. As if her heart was splitting for her father-in-law! As if you're diverting a child! But I say – how could you do it, tell me!"

"Don't talk about the guiles of unholy females, Surenda, what they can do and what they can't ... If the news came to the old man's ears, all that sari-wearing and fish eating would have to come to an end, all right."

A sudden sharp pain racked my brains.

I said, "All right *Kaka*, I'll take my leave now."

"You'll go in the dark?"

"Yes." I got off the porch.

Dinesh Roy yelled out. " I say, is your starched thread wound properly round your neck? Or have you sent it off to the washer man's, like it's the fashion in Calcutta? You'll be passing under those trees – of course, you don't believe in all that. A dead soul doesn't want to leave its own home for three days and three nights, wanders around it's own space, d'you understand?"

As I was passing under the tree, I turned in the opposite direction from home once more.

If the dead soul refuses to leave its own place and insists on wandering to death around its home for three nights and three days, then Girin Thakurda's soul must be hanging around somewhere close by. It is witnessing all these events, it can hear all these discussions.

What is the soul's reaction? Satisfied? Or is it also enraged, like all these other old rural men, and raring to rain down curses? Who knows what it wants.

I never noticed that he showed any great affection for Subhash *Kakima*. Besides since Subhash *Kaka* became obsessed by "Cinema! Cinema!" and went off to Bombay, he had become as cranky as he could possibly be, not even sparing his daughter-in-law . Of course, you couldn't really blame him.

Subhash was his last surviving child out of a total of six. If such a son also disappears from home, if his wife does not have the ability to hold him back, how can he, as the father, forgive her this inability ? How can he remain pleased with his daughter-in-law despite it?

An old father-in-law and a young daughter-in-law – this was their household. If the former, in a fit of rage, randomly hurls a heavy brass bowl of sago-and-barley and smashes the latter's forehead there's no one to hold her up.

Apparently, the first few days Subhash Kaka made a great show of writing home regularly, he even sent some money a couple of times, but for six or seven months now, there'd been no news.

No money, no letters. The household on the extreme brink of poverty. Subhash *Kakima* got the neighbouring housewives to help her sell what little gold she had.

There were no two opinions on the fact that Subhash *Kaka* was stuck in the wily web of some female illusion-monger back in Bombay.

No one in the village ever wondered how they made ends meet, but that didn't stop anyone from discussing them continuously.

A woman-being who could stand on her own strength without support, would not go to pieces even after realising that she held no attraction for her husband any more, would always talk to everyone with a smile; all this really sticks quite painfully in the eye, yet, at least it was within the bounds of tolerance. But what came to light today! That is really beyond the extreme limit.

What came to light today was this: Girin Thakurda's body was still there, the house was swarming with people, Subhash *Kakima* set down an envelope with a letter in it before all the important village elders, and said softly, " Take this letter, and read it. Then tell me what is my duty in the circumstances. If any *prayaschitt* is required, advise me about it, too."

I too, was watching all this standing on one side.

The elders picked up the letter, bursting with curiousity, quite convinced that Girin *Thakurda* had some money stashed away, the letter had something to do with it.

People pounced upon the letter at once, they paid no attention to the words that Subhash *Kakima* spoke.

The envelope had been opened, the letter was old, as soon as it was taken out, as many heads as could possibly see, swooped upon it. But was this a letter, or a burning brand?

The expressions on the faces of the elders, made those who had not read the letter even more impatient – what was it? What was up?

Summoning to his face a smile in which mockery mixed with dissatisfaction, Satish Kundu said, as he folded the letter and put it back in the envelope, "Since everyone is present here, may as well tell everything. Subhash Babaji has been dead for seven months A friend of his from Bombay had sent this news immediately after the event, but *Bouma* has seen fit to conceal this fact upto now."

Did lightning strike the room?

Concealing the news of death is in itself no novel thing. Depending upon circumtances people judge all sides of the question and do this, from time to time. But a wife concealing the news of her husband's death? What was her objective?

There was a swelling murmur amidst the crowd.

The elder stared, round eyed, open-mouthed, and an a expressionless Subhash *Kakima* began to gather together the medicine bottles, glasses, spitoons, bed clothes and clothes used during her father-in-law's illness. Finally, one of the women, I'm not sure who, said, "Yes, Satish, so what is *Bouma's* duty now?"

Satish Kundu said, "All of you decide, in all my sixty years I haven't seen such a thing, Satyadi – now unknowingly- that's different. They say that even if a snake bites you unknowingly, the poison doesn't work."

Satyadi said, "All this rubbish about sankha-sindur, the signs of her married state, maybe I'll take care of, but you do need some kind of *prayaschittir*, don't you? To knowingly break such rules, such anachar ... But tell me, *Bouma*, who gave you the idea of keeping this letter in the dark, my girl?"

Subhash *Kakima* looked up, and perhaps she even smiled a little as she said, "Who'll give me the idea, *Pishima*? It was my own ill mind, I suppose."

"Whatever it was, let me say, all this surely means something. If you thought it was a false letter, there are discerning elders in the neighbourhood whom you could've shown it to."

"But I didn't disbelieve it, *Pishima.*"

"So then?"

Subhash *Kakima* now stopped whatever she was doing, and said calmly, "I thought, *Baba* is an old man, he's suffered so much all his life, let him not suffer any more at the end of it."

"Now was that the act of any simple human being, my girl?" said Satya *Pishi.* "Everyone has come with the fruits of his own karma, there's no choice but to bear it. Now look at yourself, you stayed in his hearth for six months, knowing yourself to be a widow, a *bidhoba*, yet acting like a *sadhoba*, a married woman – do you think you did him any good by acting thus? Won't the final progress of his soul to heaven be hindered by this? Let it be now, call Bhatchaj, let's see what he says, Narayan, Narayan."

Bhatchaj appeared , also muttering Narayan, Narayan. He'd already heard everything, of course.

He expounded his views – because Girin Thakurda was her father-in-law, it would not look proper if Subhash *Kakima* being his daughter-in-law, took on widow's weeds as soon as he died. Hence let her 'final rites' be performed before his body leaves the house.

Subhash *Kakima* said, "So will any of you come with me or is it enough if I go alone?"

Satya *Pishi* said grimly, "I can see quite clearly that you don't need any help, but I have my duty, don't I? My hair's gone grey doing just this work ever since I was eighteen. Now, come.

No, no, let it be, you don't need to take your clothes or gamcha. And here Dinesh, you make whatever arrangements are necessary here."

Perhaps Satya Pishi was a little angry because even after such a major mishap, Subhash *Kakima* gave her no opportunity to cry.

All this happened in the morning. I was there only because it was a Sunday.

Now, walking in the direction opposite to that which led me home, and perhaps haunted – who can tell – by a spirit, I arrived at Girin *Thakurda's* house. It was rather late at night – it hadn't occurred to me earlier, but I realised it just as I got to Subhash *Kakima's* door.

I hesitated and was on the verge of leaving, when I saw the oil grinder Pancha Kolu's little daughter coming out to say "*Dadababu*, why are you going away? *Kakima* sent me to ask if you need anything."

I said, "No, I'd just come to see. You're staying the night here, are you?"

"Yes *Dadababu*, *Ma* sent me over she said, "The old man's dead, Banun *Didi's* all alone, Nandi go, stay the night with her."

"Isn't there anyone else from the neighbourhood."

"Why, no."

Subhash *Kakima* came out while we were talking. It's a great relief that not much of her altered clothing can be clearly made out in the moonlight.

Subhash *Kakima* is not older than me, she's not my own aunt, either, so I've never touched her feet, therefore I stood still, neither here nor there.

She said "Isn't it Monotosh? In these parts at such time?"

"I thought I'd check whether you ..."

"It's a good thing you came *bhai,*" she stopped, and smiled slightly, said, "Don't mind, I'm calling you brother, I can't say "my son" or "baba" ... Let me say – I haven't been able to say this to anyone else in the village, but I'm telling you – your *Kaka's* last rites haven't been performed, would you enquire from some Kalighat pandits whether anything can be done after so many days have passed?"

I said, "I will."

"And listen, perhaps they can give some means of atonement for my sins, some *praysachit* for me."

I said quite angrily, "Why? What do you need a *prayaschit* for?"

"I committed such an awful sin all this while. Being a *bidhoba*, and knowingly suppressing this fact to act like a married woman! Can Hindudharma bear the weight of such a terrible transgression, such *anachar*?"

"Do you consider it a sin yourself?"

"Of course I've accepted it *bhai*, all said and done, am I not the daughter of a Hindu? But my hankering for accumulating good deeds, a greed for doing *punya* had multiplied as well. I thought, why sprinkle salt on the old man's open wounds in these final days of his life? I alone can save him from the terrible grief of knowing that he's lost a son. Let me just try and over ride god's writ. So I carefully hid my own death-arrow, just like Ravan raja, staking my very life."

I said, nettled, "So what, you took it out with your own hand at the proper time, didn't you – leave aside the agony of all these days, aren't the insults you bore today enough *prayaschitt* for your sins?"

Subhash *Kakima* was quiet for a moment, then she said, "I'm not sure, I can't really understand. I think there must be some punishment. Some very harsh punishment. A terrible punishment for being able to smile, chat, walk around normally for so long ... I know that if you drink poison unknowingly, there's no sin, but what if you consume the poison knowingly? Isn't there some terribly harsh remedy for that in the *shastra*?

I couldn't think of an answer. Suddenly twelve year old Nandi brought me back to reality. "*Dada babu*, now go home. Village folk are not nice, you know, someone may be peeping from some nook or cranny and then they'll go around spreading tales. It's late, after all."

What she said was the cruel truth.

Though I blushed with embarrassment, it was difficult to turn and walk away at once without preamble. So I said, I'll ask you just one thing *Kakima*, no one is unaware of the way Girin *Thakurda* behaved with you. Yet, for his sake ..."

"Is this something to say, Monotosh?" *Kakima* could not stop herself from laughing. "He'd fly into a rage and charge at me with his stick every now and then, but does that mean I should take the responsibility of dealing him a death blow?"

"But did people understand the value of what you did?"

"People's understanding is not all there is, *bhai*."

"Alright, one more final question – I just can't get rid of this suspicion. I'm wondering, how you could do it?"

This time too, Subhash *Kakima* was silent for a while then she said, "That even I can't understand, Monotosh – how could I do it?"

Originally published in Bangla as '*Anachar*'.

Anchar can be variously rendered as custom, behaviour prompted by belief or even ritual – but *anachar* is not simply the negative from of this – rather, it implies an unjust practice, and even more, a practice that is not in accordance with that other untranslatable, nebulous term, dharma. There is, for the benefit of the non-Indian reader (an Indian reader will form her own equation with the term from her own experience) the element of infringement of religious belief regulating behaviour, or the infringement of what is right and just, an amalgamation of which may said to constitute *anachar*.

PARASURAM'S AXE

Subodh Ghosh

Translated By Sayantan Dasgupta

It was boom time for the collieries all around. More and more slums and marketplaces were coming up. It was as if the daily influx of coolies, artisans, clerks and merchants was making Nayabad froth and effervesce. As a result, Nayabad could not be called just a bazaar any longer. One police station was no longer enough to administer it. A subdivisional officer had to be deployed at Nayabad with a court. Since then, Nayabad has been a subdivision.

A few gentlemen came. The ones who came at first were some lawyers, two doctors and an overseer. A Bangla primary school was set up. A municipality also began to operate.

Long before all this, though, a beautiful church belonging to the Catholic mission had sprouted up, piercing the red soil of Nayabad. A convent for native Christian girls, an orphanage and a hospital for womenfolk. The new buildings peek out from behind the *jhau* forest, still as a painting.

Then began the series of uninterrupted changes in Nayabad. Like the night train, they pulled Nayabad across the years towards its destiny. But what most changed her identity, situation and appearance was someone called Dhania.

A short distance from Bangalitola, behind *Durgabaari*, is Dhania's mud hut, nestled next to an *aamra* tree. It has a roof made of tiles. A goat stands tied in front of the hut from dawn till dusk. The boys of the Bangla school have, therefore, named the hut *Chhagol* Lodge.

Dhania is Tilak's mother. Nobody has ever seen Tilak. Nobody knows who Tilak's father was, either. But, Tilak's younger brothers and sisters are delivered regularly every two-three years. It is as if these bloodbathed microcosms of happiness appear on life's path, silent and unnoticed, taking hold of their mother's hand. And suddenly disappear into the crowd, yanked away from her grasp. And nobody ever sees them again.

Every once in a while, Dhania disappears. No one sees her for the next two months or so. During that time, we can find her in a free bed in the mission hospital for the womenfolk. A tiny nondescript human baby lies curled up near her breast. It grows for a few days in her warm, soft arms. The flaccid body begins to fill out a little, the folds and lines in its skin gradually begin to smoothen out. It blinks its eyes every now and then, flails its arms and legs. A little touch, and the hungry lips part like the leaves of a young sapling.

After that, no more. The bird flies away and Dhania returns alone to her *Chhagol* Lodge. And Tilak's brothers, too, routinely move into the mission orphanage. Dhania is a curious character. The nurses at the hospital cannot help being surprised. The dumbfounded lady doctor, too, says, "Jesus! I'm really stunned. This girl has turned both my Bible and my science topsy-turvy. I thought the baby birds flew away when they grew up. This is the first time I've seen the bird itself fly, abandoning the baby."

Dhania's lodge skirts the gentlefolk's neighbourhood. She has no relatives. Nobody to socialise with. But all this is only till sunset; it becomes irrelevant after dusk.

If you stand on the road at night, you will sense an odd world at dalliance at the hut under the *aamra* tree – something that takes place through whispers alone. Hazy darkness, muffled laughter. The only sound here is a whisper; the only music here is a vague humming. Everything is nebulous and ill-defined. Nobody is seen coming here; nor does anybody ever leave. No one, apart from the policemen on the round, knows the reality of those invisible shadow-lives. But there's never any uproar over it. For the constable on the round, the opportunity to earn opens up as many times as Dhania's door opens at night.

That was the way things were going. But why is Dhania discussed in decent circles? Not many can forget Dhania.

The boys remember Dhania on their way home after the Bangla school gets over. They head for the *aamra* tree near *Chhagol* Lodge. Their whole waiting day would remain unfulfilled without being abused by Dhania and without having garnered a few aamras with their pebbles.

The Dhania topic comes up in the evening conversation among the lawyers and the doctor *babus* at the clubhouse. The girl has nobody, yet she manages all right, they say. *Something's wrong.*

The constables on duty brighten up as soon as they pop a bit of tobacco into their mouths before they take up their posts at ten. The boredom of all-night watch. The few minutes of relaxation in the sweet darkness in front of the *aamra* tree are a welcome break. The faint flicker of a lamp from inside Dhania's room – the heavenly glow of earnings and reward. They don't even look at the moonlit sky with so much enthusiasm.

And that's not all. The shadow of Dhania's persona has spread far; it has penetrated into the sacred interiors of the decent Bengali family. This, of course, has happened out of sheer necessity. Things came to such a pass that even the community of young mothers had no option but to bank on the help of Dhania, the glory of their motherhood otherwise threatened to die out on them.

New mothers from decent well-off families all seemed to be suffering from one illness or the other. Someone was plagued by puerperal ailment, someone was shrinking in anaemia, someone else had seen the fountain inside her breasts dry up.

The lady doctor from the Mission Hospital charged a hefty fee and went from house to house examining the new mothers and voicing her opinion – the mothers could continue with their treatment, but no treatment would succeed on the babies. They needed vitality, not medicine.

"The solution, then?"

"A strong, healthy, ayah to feed the babies breast-milk."

Fear and anxiety replaced happy smiles in many a home. The need to tackle this threat to the family line paved the way for Dhania's entrance, straight from the *aamra* tree into the labour room and the interiors of decent homes.

Dhania has to answer the call of many houses. The part-time breast-feeder. The twice-a-day rate is six rupees a month, a daily quarter-seer payment of rice and a new saree when she's about to leave on the day her part-time job gets over. Dhania works her way from house to house under these conditions.

Dhania leaves for her part-time job just before dawn and returns by dusk every day. She carries a clean, folded towel in her hand. An ever-present smile on her face. Hair smelling of lemon-scented oil and tied up neatly. A thin washed saree over a red petticoat. When she walks, the silver bells on her toes ring and produce a sound like the popping of corn. She wears a gold nose stud shaped like clubs – it gels well with the flickering smile playing on her lips. It's the neatness rather than the toilet that strikes you. But she does look pretty – on a sudden encounter, one finds her showy.

Dhania entered the inner quarters of Ghoshalbabu's house. She has to work part-time once a day here. There's a baby boy, just three years old.

As soon as she spotted her, the maid screwed up her face and went inside. Ghoshalbabu's thin and tattered wife sits on a *mora,* a wicker stool. The new-born baby lies asleep in a swing nearby.

"There, she's arrived!" the maid went in and reported. "What pride! The skin crawls in repulsion."

Ghoshalbabu's wife pacified the rebellious maid. "Let her be. Don't tell her anything to her face, maid. It's an emergency; we need her services. What does it matter to us, what kind of a person one really is?"

Dhania advances towards the swing, puts the baby to her breast, and sits down. She asks a few inane questions. "How are you today, *didi*?" She notices the niggardliness of the replies and doesn't speak too much after that. She waits for a while after the job is done. Ties the payment up in the *gamchhaa*, her cheap cloth towel, and moves on.

In the evening, a group of women meet at Narenbabu's house. Dhania arrives. She has to feed a grown-up boy there. A three-year-old lean and thin boy – his stomach cannot yet digest cow's milk. He drives everybody at home crazy with his older-than-his-years looks and his violent behaviour. He cries and throws tantrums all the time he is awake. No sympathy or promise has had any effect on him.

Dhania climbed up to the verandah and clapped her hands: "*Aaao, mera laal*".

The boy, who had been rolling on the ground and yelling his head off, raised his hood like an entranced snake and ran quickly to Dhania, jumped onto her lap. He fidgeted for some time with Dhania's armlets. Then he curled himself up and quietly lay down on her breasts.

Some time later, Dhania called out, "The boy has gone to sleep. Where do I lay him down?"

Suddenly, the girls in the room became animated as if touched by the wisp of an amusing thought. Together, they cornered Narenbabu's wife. "Quick, hurry up and answer. Haven't you heard what the boy's new mother has asked?"

Caught on the wrong foot, Naranbabu's wife feels disgraced and irritated and loses her temper. "I'm not going to talk to her or do anything of the sort. Puti, you go and bring *Khoka.*"

So, Puti, the eight-year-old simpleton daughter of the overseer*babu*, has to go forward.

Dhania is waiting for her payment. In the meantime, the others peek at her. She has walked such a long distance, yet her feet are so clean. As if dirt and grime have rolled off her feet.

Some blurt out the wrong things – "The bitch's hands are so delicate. The amulet has eaten into her flesh".

The curious glances and peeks stopped as soon as Dhania disappeared outside the back door. The Master's wife spoke through her nose and let out a couple of shudders. "I'm never going to wear a red petticoat again. Never in my life!"

In the afternoon, Dhania can be seen sitting on a *mora* outside her hut and smoking away. An episode of cootchie-cooing ensues between Dhania, who speaks in a voice dripping with love and affection, and the goat, which grazes on the grass nearby.

But Dhania hasn't been seen in the last few days. The door to her mud hut near the *aamra* tree is bolted. Dhania's goat is tied in front of another hut near the *nullah* – old Prosadi Dom's hut.

Prosadi is around eighty. He had been sentenced to *kaalapani,* the Andamans, on a dacoity charge once, when he was eighteen. Though he had been released, since then, he had gone to jail five times for theft. Forty-two of his years have been spent consuming prison food. He had forgotten the ways of earning his own food by the time he was free. But the greatest blow was yet to come. A tree snapped in a storm and fell and broke his waist. Since then, he has never walked.

Then, there are the old-age symptoms spread all over his body. Prosadi has been alive, just waiting for death. Now, he looks like hunger itself, waiting with extended jaws. He is

Dhania's only pet, apart from the goat. Once she is done with cooking, she reaches a plate of rice everyday to Prosadi. That was probably why he lived on.

Dhania's goat stood outside Prosadi's house.

The evening lights have come on at the hospital for the womenfolk. The nurses crowd around Dhania's bed. Everybody voices the same request: "At least, keep this baby."

"No, Miss sister, I can't."

Lady doctor: "Who hasn't heard of your sullied reputation? You won't be able to keep it covered up. So, why not keep him?"

"No, *Ladydoctorji*, I won't be able to feed him and clothe him. He will suffer hardships and will turn into my enemy when he grows up. I don't have the money to bring up a son."

"What mad things are you saying! Even the beggar girls don't abandon their sons. It's not as if they have a lot of money, is it?"

"They don't raise their sons, Sister; they turn them into beggars. I can't do that."

"Okay, we'll all pool in some money. Take the boy with you."

"In that case, why don't one of you take the boy home? I'll be there as your ayah in any case."

The lady doctor and the nurses don't carry on with the argument. Even they shudder when they look into Dhania's eyes. They, too, trade on charity and mercy, but Dhania's quiet indifference appears cruel and in bad taste to them.

"Adab! I'll leave now."

Dhania gets up. A nurse wraps Dhania's son in a piece of flannel and picks him up – he'll be sent to the Nursery. Dhania doesn't care; she ties up her brass plate and pot in her towel, and, picking up the hurricane lantern, gets up.

Another nurse walks in with the Register. Lady Doctor asks, "What's the kid's pop's name?"

Dhania: "That I don't know."

The lady doctor gets incensed. "Those same words again and again. Why don't you just name the person you live with now?"

"I live with several people; and I don't even know the names of many of them. You must forgive me, *Ladydoctorji*. Put down any name you can think of."

"Your future is bleak. Very bleak."

The lady doctor walks off, sulking.

The mail train has just left Nayabad station and is speeding up. The hospital building is shaking. Dhania descends the stairs, a red quilt wrapped round her. Some undefinable emotion fogs the nurses' eyes.

The durwan rang the hour just as Dhania crossed the threshold. Nine p.m.

Years have passed by one after the other. The rhythm of

Dhania's life under the *aamra* tree hasn't been at all interrupted. Only, she had had to go to the hospital for womenfolk for the last time three years or so ago.

The Nayabad municipality has been flourishing. There has been a planned extension to the town. Seven hundred and forty-one was the number of the car the lawyerbabu has bought.

Five, seven, ten, twelve, sixteen – the years have rolled by one after the other. Dhania is almost in her forties now. Occasionally, she lights an uncovered oven on the streetside and sells *telebhaja,* cheap snacks fried in oil. Coolies buy some of her stuff on their way home from work in the evenings. She prepares a basket or two of cowdung cakes too once in a while; it all gets sold off. The glow is absent in her appearance; and the absence of money is even more evident. It's a rare night these days when one can hear a man's voice under the *aamra* tree. But she has her body; she has her health. So, Dhania is not afraid. She knows she won't have to beg.

Dhania's excursions into gentle society have stopped long ago. New mothers have improved their health. There's no need for a part-time breast feeder now. Besides, several competitors have arrived for Dhania from across the seas – umpteen kinds of foreign food. Dhania isn't called anymore these days to moisten the drying-up lifespan of new-born babies. It seems as if everybody has forgotten her.

It's the Christmas holidays. Patna's schools and colleges are closed. The boys have returned home. It's the season of hunts, picnics, carnivals and exhibitions. The blood pumps faster to a more exciting beat in Nayabad's veins. That day, the fire remained unlit in Dhania's home. She was totally broke. The incidents of so long ago came to her mind and created a colourful picture in front of her eyes.

Dhania sat up. "Let me go and drop in at the babus' houses. I used to work for them once, after all. One can ask for a bonus." If they were pleased, if she could raise even ten rupees...

Dhania couldn't enter inside Narenbabu's house. Ghoshalbabu gave her four annas. Dhania stared – the house was full of children. The boys have become so tall.

Another house. Here, her entry is less rigidly barred. The woman of the house gave her some money and said: "You've got what you will, sweetheart. Now, off you go, quick."

After she had waited for an hour at the gate of Dhirenbabu's house, the maid came and handed her a rupee. "Ma has sent this. Now, get out of here."

Dhania: "Maid didi, where is the eldest son?" The maid looked at her suspiciously for some time and then said, "There, playing cards. But, what business is all that of yours?"

"Oooh, he's become so grown-up." He wouldn't let go of her tits even after his teeth had come out. "He bit me once and put me in such a spot, do you remember, maid?"

"I don't like such pretensions, I tell you. You, go. Don't come this way again."

So many houses are still left. But there was something that began to bother Dhania. This is hardly a bonus she is receiving. This is probably what is called begging. There's still a fair bit of daylight to go. But Dhania walked quickly back home.

But that wasn't the end of it. Maids and mistresses raised complaints and objections in their homes. "Where did that *Rahu* appear from again? So many eligible young men in the area. Who knows when the bitch will go and spoil somebody's life?"

The masters of the houses listened. Not a totally unfounded fear. These creatures shouldn't be allowed in the vicinity. Their presence is an open invitation to goons and anti-socials.

The matter was also taken up in the evening gathering at the club. Everybody agreed with the proposal. The depravity under the *aamra* tree near the *Durgabaari* must be weeded out.

The sound of a band. Dhania relinquished the hookah and stood up. Sounds like the boys from the Mission orphanage marching their way to a picnic. Blue-blazer, half-pants and white flannel shirts. Red socks and boots on their feet. A platoon of charity-fed young men between five and sixteen. It's their band party ahead of the procession. The band's uniform is different. They have velvet hats on their head, white feathers and young *jhau* leaves pinned onto them. Small bagpipe reeds stuck in their shapely lips. Tiny drums dangling from straps across their shoulders.

The glow of the Christmas sun has only just conquered the fog and has begun to frolic on the roads and the fields. The procession stopped near the crossing in the road. The bagpipes and drums raised three final warning beats and fell silent. A curious crowd – boys, girls, old men – came from all directions and surrounded them.

A Father in a dazzling white overall and white pantaloons sang the Hindi version of a hymn to David.

"Amen!"

The chorus of the boys' voices! A sound like the whistling of the wind in the jungle, a sound like the crescendo of the waterfall, a sound like the music of the birds at dawn. Dhania was mildly disconcerted. She walked closer to the procession and stood there, leaning against a tree.

The tall, bearded Fathers look as if they're straight out of the jungle. Another Father gave a speech, his cross glinting on his chest. "Nineteen hundred and forty years ago, the sun had risen over Bethlehem on a morning like this. A poor carpenter woman gave birth to the Son of Man."

It's hard to catch the drift of the Father's speech. Dhania shifts her position slightly so that she can see the faces of the boys clearly.

"Wearing a crown of thorns, the Son of Man walks the streets of Jerusalem, ready to sacrifice himself to redeem you and me."

Dhania's gaze was now tasting the features of every boy like some unseen kiss. At least six of them were hers. But there's no way of telling which ones. That ten-year-old drummer boy wiping his face on the sleeve of his shirt – perhaps he is one of them. Or, maybe the one next to him. But, then, who is not? It seems everyone is one of them.

Dhania stood as if in a trance. The crowd has dispersed long ago. The fog near the top of the distant trees has melted. The procession marches through the field. Dust rises. All earthly dust has turned sweet.

Leaving the support of the tree trunk, Dhania began to retrace her steps homewards, slowly, tired. It was as if a wondrous sense of exhaustion and pleasure had spread all over her body and had drained away, just like an orgasmic flood of sensations. Dhania pulled her *aanchal*, the end of her saree, carefully over her breast. Her corset was wet.

Municipal Commissioners' meeting. An important notice was sent to the constabulary chief officer. "Let all the lower-caste fallen women who secretly practice their disreputable trade in various well-off quarters of the city be segregated and shifted to the bazaar lines."

Strict government orders. It's the responsibility of the Town thana police. They will have to draw up a list of such wasted women and then rehabilitate them to the bazaar area.

It didn't take much time for the order to make its impact felt on Dhania's world under the *aamra* tree. "No more. Move on yourself, or you'll be moved. Or, stay on the right path."

Dhania didn't leave any stone unturned to hold on. She pleaded and prayed, coaxed and cajoled. She offered to sell her belongings and bribe the town police with thirty rupees for their 'paan (betel leaf) expenses'. Let her be spared, in return. Nothing doing, said the constables – this time, there's no way out. "We, too, have to make sure that we don't lose our jobs. You'll have to register."

"Forget all your schemes and plots this time," the head constable reprimanded. "Come, put your thumb impression here."

Night. Prosadi was sitting in front of the still-glowing embers, head tucked between his knees. The fire is getting colder. The dog is growling loudly near him. Prosadi is oblivious to it. A piece of burning ember has scalded and scorched the little toe of his left foot. But he doesn't feel any pain. He has been shivering since morning. Now, even that throb of life is absent. Dhania hasn't come these last two days. He hasn't had a single morsel.

"Prosadi *chacha,*" Dhania arrived and began to sob. Prosadi still didn't respond. Dhania now gave the old man a good hard knock, shook him, and pulled his face up by his chin. "Prosadi *chacha,*" she called out again as the old man opened his eyes. Dhania is weeping. The anguish of these tears touched Prosadi like the stroke of lightning. The body woke up in a hurry. "What's this? You, Dhania?"

"Yes, *chacha*. I have no caste, they say, I'm a whore."

"Shame! What are you saying?"

"Yes, *chacha*. I had to write my name. I'll have to stay in the bazaar from tomorrow."

"Oh, no! You are Lachhmi, the goddess".

"No, *chacha*. I don't have a husband."

"No cow has a husband. Does that mean it's not Lachhmi?"

"But I'm not a cow."

Dhania suddenly stood up. "I have to leave, *chacha*. I don't know if we'll ever meet again."

Like a worthless son, Prosadi looked hungrily this way and that. The familiar *gamchha* that used to cover the plate of rice – his life-saver – was absent from Dhania's hands. Perhaps Prosadi was about to say something, but the words never came out. He plunged his head between his knees again as if in silent sadness. He heard once again the commotion of the *kalapaani*, lost to the shore.

Dhania was standing. Absent-mindedly, she let the saree drop from her head, bunched her hair together and tied it into a tight little bun. She wiped her greasy face once with her *aanchal*. Then, her face began to glow with her ever-familiar flickering smile.

"You're mad at me, *chacha*." Dhania slowly moved closer to him and lifted the helpless unfeeling figure of the decrepit Prosadi onto her lap as if he were a kitten. Taking her corset off, she pressed Prosadi's head to her bosom. She began slowly to unknot the matted grey hair on the old man's head.

An hour has passed. A satiated Prosadi has fallen asleep. Dhania is wet and exhausted.

We are in a wide alley to the south of Chowkbazaar. Rows of two-storeyed buildings line the two sides. Just around the middle of this stretch stand two shops on opposite sides. One sells Indian liquor, the other, foreign liquor. All the ground-floor rooms are shops – they sell paan, beedi, attar, sherbet, chaat and chameli oil. Broken tablas and pakhwajes are repaired at one shop. Eunuchs can be seen clapping and dancing on a paved platform around a tree close by. The upstairs windows begin to glitter like pieces of a larger bioscope screen as soon as it is dusk. The rows of those who sell their beauty and their bodies.

The New Year saw a new window open on the first floor.

Her life and her youth have been purified by the fire of forty years; all impurities have been destroyed. Dhania dressed the way she wanted to.

Lighting the chandelier, Dhania made a bun near the top of her head. She wrapped a golden glittery handkerchief over that. She put on a necklace of false pearls. Wrapped a thin blue saree round her waist, not caring to put on a petticoat. Sprinkled fistfuls of powder over her body. Chewed on *paan* with strong *zarda* to paint her lips red. Warmed her throat by gulping down a neat a mug of country liquor. Put on a green velvet corset that hugged her tightly. Dhania rested her elbows on the bars of the half-grilled window, bent forward and stood still and confident.

The winter-evening air has become heavy with the smoke and the smell of fried papads from the sweetshop. A handful of people stand near the gas post on the street below and stare at the window.

Doesn't matter if it is night, if one is intoxicated, or if the moonlight gets charred by the gas light. They can always be recognised. Ghoshalbabu's stocky eldest son is exhaling regular, agitated puffs of cigarette smoke. The cashier's son, the boy with the guilty eyes, is trying to signal something with his handkerchief. A drunkard also totters up and joins the group. Rounding his palms in front of an eye and holding them there like a telescope, he finds his target and stands there for some time.

Dhania swallowed a gulp of the red *paan* juice. Her ears have become hot and have started to sweat. She let her *aanchal* fall back from her shoulder. Dhania raised her two arms above her head, clutched the window frame and shoved her breasts out between the bars.

The crowd sees stars. A colourful, semi-nude mirage burns brightly at the window. The shadowy lure of two ripe thighs behind the transparent silk saree. Further upwards are a pair of fresh, full, mischievously restless planets, forever captured in the depths of her corset.

A terrible happiness burned through her entire body and

made Dhania restless. Still, she waits quietly. She will stand here till midnight, till the wee hours of the morning – until the first *babu* of her new life comes and knocks on her door and calls her by her new name.

Originally published in Bangla as *Parasuram-er kuthar*.

LORD OF THE FORESTS

Joytirindra Nandi

Translated By Sayantan Dasgupta

Trees talk to me".

"The branches? Or the leaves?"

"Branches, leaves, flowers, buds, fruits, all – they all whisper to me."

"Will they speak to me?"

"Of course they will!" Sarada reaches for his grandson's hand and draws him close. Then, pressing his small head against the trunk of a badaam tree, he smiled quietly, "Now listen carefully, you'll hear it speak."

Moti does just that. He stands still, pressing his ear against the thick bark that covered the lower part of the huge tree trunk The robust and restless summer wind makes the young green badaam leaves rustle, and scurries off in the other direction. Moti's hair is doing a jig. Sarada is bald; he doesn't have any hair, his grey moustache quivers slightly in the wind, but it is his lips which quiver so much more eloquently, The quivering of his lips has nothing to do with the wind. Moti realizes that Dadu's (grandfather's), lips are quivering because he is trying to hold his laughter silently down somewhere in his throat. This is Dadu's prankishness. Moti wonders sometimes if there are other old men and women who are as fond of pranks as Dadu is.

"Did you hear anything?"

"No," Moti shook his head, frowning, and removed his ear from the tree trunk. "I hear nothing."

"Waaak-ptoooie," Sarada turns the other way and spits on the tapioca jungle beside the mound of soil. He doesn't smile this time. His lips are still behind his moustache. The badaam tree is swaying too much in the restless wind; so, the *holdibona* bird leaves its branch and flies off. As if following the flight of the holdibona, Sarada let out a deep sigh. Then he lowers his eyes and looks at his grandson's face.

"Your ear's gone bust. Living in the city's done this to you, my boy."

"Has it?"

He muses over something as he looks at the grey-yellow balls of Dadu's eyes. Then, Moti bares his row of milk-white teeth and smiles. "Why, we have a guava tree at our Beadon Street house – such a large gulmohar tree on the road – how come they don't speak?

"Beadon Street trees...?" Sarada makes a disgusting noise with his throat as he utters these words. "The ghrrr-ghrrr sound of cars twenty-four hours a day; do those trees have anything left, the way they have to listen to the screams of the radio? They've all gone dumb. Talk? Forget it; they're too busy just trying to keep themselves alive and their hearts beating on." Sarada ejects another mass of spit from his mouth. "What is the lifespan of your guava and gulmohar trees on Beadon Street?"

Moti is silent.

"Here, trees have nothing but other trees near them. So much of grass and soil near the roots. And, look there, how each tree is affectionately embraced by *aparajita*, *lata*, *jhumkolata*."

Moti stares open-mouthed at the trees and the dense vegetation all around him. Sarada points to the branches of various trees.

"And, variously-coloured birds alight on the branches, between the leaves, sing, sharpen their beaks on the stems of the leaves; they peck at the fruits, don't they?" Dadu's grey-yellow eyeballs flicker with excitement. The grandson nods his head and says faintly, "Yes."

Sarada's full, dark lips suddenly arc again behind his moustache. "And what's there near the roots of your trees on Beadon Street? Stone chips, molten pitch, electric wires tie up the trees, four-storeyed, two-storeyed buildings tower above the tree tops."

The grandson again nods and agrees in a faint voice. Silently digs at the grass in the soil with his toe nails.

"So, the trees in the city do not talk. They've had so much of petrol fumes to drink that their tongues have dropped out. Listening to the ghrrr-ghrrr of cars and the screams of the radio has made their ears lose their sharpness." Sarada ends his discourse and spits into the tapioca jungle.

"Do trees have ears, Dadu?"

"Of course, they do. They have tongues, they have ears. They have noses, they have eyes." Dadu nods his head solemnly.

"They can see everything like we do?"

Moti widens his shiny, black eyes and looks all around him. Sarada walks on. Moti walks on too. The two leave the tapioca jungle behind them and walk down the sloping land. It's rained rather heavily last night. Knee-high water has collected there. The two of them have barely reached the edge of the water, they have barely dipped their legs in the water, when two-three hundred frogs dispersed from somewhere with a jump and leapt into the water. Though he was scared at first, later Moti found it amusing. He clapped his hands and shouted in glee.

"Why don't you stuff a dozen or two into your pant pocket?" Dadu suggests seriously. "Look at their oily, yellow bodies."

"Hunnnhh! What'll I do with them?" Moti wrinkles his nose.

"You'll eat them fried and made into *charchari*".

"Waaak-ptoooie," Moti spits in disgust. "The Chinese eat frogs. Why should we do it?"

"Yes, you'll only have rotten fish preserved in ice for days. You've become all-bones-and-nothing-else because you've been having rotten, stale fish. One can count all your ribs."

It's true. Moti's health has deteriorated. That is why he has come here as soon as school closed for the summer, responding to Dadu's letter. He's feeling much better in this last week or so. He's been having fresh fish from the pond and pure, unadulterated milk here.

The two of them crossed the flooded field and reached their destination. Not one, but seven-eight *jaam* trees. Their outspread branches have cast a deep shadow over the place. And bunches of black *jaam* dangle above their heads. As if innumerable ragged clouds of the *Sravan* sky have come and made their home near the treetops. Moti stares in wonder. He has never seen so many ripe *jaam*s together. Not all of them have matured, though. Young, unripe, green ones – half-ripened red *jaam*s on the tree – even that is nothing to sneer at. It's as if somebody has slung garlands of red, green and black pebbles at the top of the branches.

"What are you looking at, wonder-struck like that?" Dadu shouts at him.

"Just looking. It looks beautiful".

"Yes!" Sarada suddenly laughs as if struck by a funny thought. "Looks beautiful. If you stand below the tree quietly, will the fruit jump into your mouth?"

"No, they won't", Moti shakes his head.

"That's your problem – beautiful, beautiful." Sarada takes the *gamchha* from his shoulders and wraps it round his waist.

Like Moti, he, too, wears shorts. Bare body, bare legs. Doesn't matter that he's old, the flesh of his arms and legs is as tough as rock. Dadu lives in the village, that's why he is so healthy, Moti thinks. And, in comparison, Moti's father, yes, Sukumarbabu, the son of this very Sarada Ray, his body has become soft and flabby. Moti now remembered his father's figure. It's eleven now. His father has gone to office. His office is in a huge, red building on Dalhousie Square. One day Moti had accompanied their servant and had visited his office. Moti thought if his father came to the village he too would become as healthy as his grandfather. Moti even wondered whether or not to give father that advice when he returned to Calcutta this time. But Ma wouldn't come even if Baba wanted to. Moti is sure of it. Ma had raised major objections to his trip here. Snakes, frogs, jungles, mud and water – there's nothing else here. It's impossible for a decent person to live in a village. Besides, you'd have only stupid farmers for company. Perhaps, their children would be Moti's only companions. He won't hear a good word, won't be in touch with his studies, he'll spend his days and nights wandering about the fields and jungles and will come back having mastered how to steal birds' young and to control cows and goats. Of course, in spite of Ma's objections, Baba had, after getting Dadu's letter, sent him here with an escort. Moti likes it here. Farmers, snakes and frogs, jungle, mud – there is a lot more here, a lot more that is really nice, really beautiful. Moti wishes he could stay here forever, not just during the summer holidays. If only his parents, too, could come here.

Sarada will move past sixty nine and will step into seventy this *Aswin*. He extends his hand, tears a bunch of *kalojaam* and puts it into the folds of the *gamchha* at his waist before wondering if he has been able to earn the admiration of his ten-year-old grandson by climbing onto the top branch. He pops four or five *jaam*s into his mouth. Ten or twelve *jaam*s get separated from the bunch and roll down onto the ground. Moti begins gathering them gleefully. When the caverns of Sarada's mouth become full of the nectary-sour juice and pulp of ripe, plump *jaam,* his eyeballs begin to shine like the pupils of a small boy's eyes, the hazy, yellow colour disappears and his eyes become bright red like the seeds of a ripe *jaam*.

"Looks beautiful, that's what you're obsessed with, that's your problem." Sarada tries to climb up to the top branch. "What looks good also tastes good. But you people have forgotten to eat." Sitting atop the top branch, Sarada talks to Moti in his mind. "Your Beadon Street house has curtains to match the pattern of your sofa covers; it has potted flowers. It has a radio, neon lights, dressing table, china utensils, plastic toys crowding the rooms. Your mother doesn't wear in the evening the saree she wore in the morning; she takes off the beautiful saree-blouse she wore in the morning and drives herself crazy, wondering which one is more beautiful, which one would suit her better. Your father spends his days with his beautiful, tie, suit, shoes, car, his fashionable valet and peon. No, I won't say you starve. Sukumar sits under the fan in a closed, glass-partitioned office chamber and lunches on bread, tinned butter, two boiled potatoes, kept alive in Sealdah's cold-storage chambers, pepper, stale eggs, some dry boiled vegetables and a large barfi made of milk powder. Balanced diet? Who will deny it? Following the instructions of a top city doctor to the letter, Sukumar sits in his office, and has his well-balanced afternoon meal comprising proteins, fat, carbohydrates and minerals, as he runs his eyes through a newspaper. At home, Sukumar's wife has just lunched on fish curry and *charchari* cooked with adulterated oil, turmeric powder and chilli powder and is burping and thinking which cinema hall in the city has a good film running this week, perhaps she'll go for a matinee show. Cinema? Sarada twisted his face as he thought about it. And quickly popped a *jaam*, double the normal size, into his mouth. "You live in the city with the life span of a mortal human being. Obsessed with external appearances and flourishes. But, what is the adulterated food and the poisoned air doing to your life span ...?"

Moti begins to shout from below, "Dadu, why are you climbing so high? If the branch breaks ..."

Sarada laughs. Sits atop the high branch and looks down.

"The branch will tell me before it breaks. It'll make a cracking sound to warn me. But, the traffic on your Beadon Street crawls onto you without giving any warning."

Moti falls silent. The group of magpies and bulbulis of this tree, driven away by Dadu, fly into another tree and raise a hue and cry; they begin to peck at the ripe *jaams*. But old Dadu is not far behind either, Moti muses. Only this morning, before leaving the house, he had eaten a huge bowl of *kheer-muri* with four ripe mangoes. Now, again, he has climbed onto the tree and is devouring ripe *jaams* to his heart's content. He must already have finished 110-150 of them. Moti can't eat too many. "Your stomach has shrunk and withered away, city boy, what stuff can you really digest and, how much?" Dadu was teasing him in the morning. Because Thakuma, his grandmother, had condensed the milk into such wonderful kheer last night; Moti could only have that much, and no more! The smell of the kheer is still on his fingers. Moti is discovering here what the smell of milk, the smell of kheer, the smell of ghee is. "Keep eating, and you'll gradually discover you can eat more." Listening to Dadu's teasing, Thakuma was telling Moti, "Eating is a matter of habit – how much could you eat in Calcutta? Now, it even astonishes me sometimes to see how much you eat." Dadu was smiling. "You're astonished or you're afraid? – out with the truth." As if as a result of Dadu's scoffing, Thakuma was silent in embarrassment. But Dadu wasn't silent. "Yes, one should get worried, the way my paunch is growing – one must be careful about the eating if one is to extend one's life span. Otherwise, if the thread suddenly snaps, if, all of a sudden, I die of thrombosis, or something like it, will you become braver?" Listening to this, Thakuma was saying, enraged, "Aah! What words! Why, how old are you, anyway, that you are speaking such nonsense?" Without saying anything else, Dadu has begun to concentrate on eating mangoes and kheer, and Thakuma has poured some more kheer into Dadu's bowl. Looking at Dadu's and Thakuma's eyes together, Moti understood that Thakuma gets as much pleasure in seeing him eat as Dadu gets eating.

Life span? As he remembered the words, Moti thought about his father. No, his father can hardly eat. Baba has just this much rice, a couple of *luchi*s, or this much of *suji*, and raises both his hands and forbids Ma to give him anything else. As if Baba's belly would burst if he had a *lúchi* or a handful of rice more. This is not a good sign, Moti now understands as he observes Dadu and listens to him; maybe, one day, his father will ...

"Here, come one ..."

Moti is startled. Dadu has come down from the tree. He has so many *jaam*s tied around his waist. His hairy paunch seems to have swelled with the juice of the fruits.

"I can't eat any more, Dadu," Moti shakes his head.

"You just had the few you picked from the ground, and that has satisfied your hunger? Have the ones from the tree, at least a few." Sarada smiled and handed a handful of *jaams* to his grandson. Moti doesn't say no again. He pops a *jaam* or two into his mouth and walks at Dadu's side.

"So, you've seen my *jaam* garden, you've seen my mango garden – next, I'll show you my *jaamrul* and guava gardens."

Moti was pleased, and he began to walk faster. He had seen Dadu's mango garden yesterday; today, he's seen his *jaam* garden.

"You've planted all the trees, Dadu?"

Sarada spat again. His spit is dark blue, thanks to the juice of the *jaam*. "The *jaam* trees were already there. It was because I saw that there were so many jaam trees together here that I bought the land on this side too."

"Mango – you were saying yesterday you'd planted all the mango trees."

"Yes," Sarada looks up at the sky. "There wasn't a single mango tree when I came here. I had to buy a thousand rupees' worth of mango grafts and plant them. That's how I have such a big garden now."

"The mangoes in your garden are rather good."

"Nothing but *himsagar* and *mohanphuli* was planted, my

boy. I'm very choosy when it comes to mangoes. I can't stand bad mangoes." Sarada averts his gaze from the sky and looks back at his grandson. The boy seems to be thinking about something. He is sweating and his face has turned bright red.

"How come you're laughing?" Sarada raises his eyebrows. A grey hair or two remains in his eyebrows; the rest of the hair has dropped off, and, his forehead seems to be looking broader than it did previously. Drops of sweat settle into the two-three canals on his forehead and glitter in the sunshine. "Last year, I planted five hundred-rupees' Singapore bananas and pineapples."

"I've seen the banana garden, but I haven't seen the pineapple garden." Moti gulped.

"One by one, you'll see them all. Now that you've come here, you'll see them all – orange, guava, kamranga, jaamrul, sabeda – you'll see all the gardens."

Moti's eyes flashed with excitement.

"I love to eat sabedas".

Sarada doesn't say anything; he walks on. Moti walks on, too. They turned the bend round a large pond and again came to a world of giant shadows, where lots of branches and leaves lay strewn on the ground. Moti counted. Four trees in each row, twelve *jaamrul* trees in all in the three rows. There seem to be more fruits than leaves on some of the trees. Numerous nice and plump, milk-white *jaamruls* can be seen dangling behind the dense green leaves. There are more birds here than on the *jaam* trees. They are more active here, more eloquent. The parrot, the bulbuli, the magpie, the crow – they like the milky *jaamrul* more than the black *jaam*s, Moti realised. And squirrels? With puffed-up tails, they rush from this branch to that.

"How does it look to you, Moti? Do you like it?"

"Really nice – looks like the trees have stars blooming on them."

"Poetry?" Sarada made a face. He spat. Then he reaches out and tears a bunch of *jaamrul*s from a drooping branch and hands it to his grandson. "Taste it – how sweet and juicy my fruits are."

"Very sweet." Moti bites into a fruit. But Sarada is not waiting to hear his grandson's response. Reaching out and tearing another bunch of *jaamrul*s, he pops them one by one into his mouth and chews on them. The juice flows down the side of Sarada's mouth as if he were a little boy, and stops at the end of his elbow and hangs there, suspended. Moti finds it amusing. Moti has understood after coming here that his sixty-year-old Dadu is but a tyke. He's finding it difficult to finish one *jaamrul*. Dadu is finishing off five; he is extending his life span. Moti thinks about it and laughs to himself.

"We'll go to see the pineapple fields now, shall we?"

"No, no," Sarada shakes his head and says, "pineapple fields, at this time of the year? They are still green – the pineapples will start ripening only after a shower or two. They're all unripe now."

It's not just a matter of seeing the fruit orchards; there's an undeniable link between seeing and eating, Sarada tries again and again to tell Moti. Moti understands and doesn't talk of pineapples again. But, though he doesn't say anything, he mulls over some thing and keeps smiling faintly every now and then.

"What makes you smile?"

"I want to give you a name."

"What name?" Sarada is pleased. He looks at his grandson's shiny eyes. "Come on, tell me."

"Lord of the fruits," Moti chortled.

"Hunh, even better, call me 'Lord of the trees', 'Lord of the orchards', perhaps." Sarada munches on the last *jaamrul* in his hand. "The fruit comes later, the tree is first, understand?" Sarada thinks up something amusing and laughs to himself. "Then, last season, I couldn't have a single mango, you know?"

Moti stares at Dadu, mystified.

"Last season, the storms ruined all the young mangoes. Such a huge mango orchard, and not a single mango could ripen here."

"Then?"

"What, then? Fine, I didn't have a ripe mango, so what? That didn't mean I'd get mad at the trees in my orchard or wouldn't nurse them. Rather, last season, I spent most of my time in my barren mango orchard. The *jaam*s in the *jaam* orchard there ripened and dropped off onto the ground, the ripe *jaams* formed a knee-deep carpet on the grass, but I didn't go that way even once. Yes, all the jaamrul trees became white with *jaamrul.* Squrrels and hordes and hordes of birds had their fill of *jaamruls;* I didn't even come to take a peek."

"Then you love the trees more than you love the fruits," Moti said hesitantly. "Then...?" Sarada made a noise with his nose. "How many fruits do I have, anyway? Have I planted so many trees so that I alone can eat? The birds eat my fruits more, the bats and squirrels eat my fruits more – there they go."

"I can see that." Sarada's city-bred ten-year-old grandson watches the activity of the puffed-tail squirrels on the trees and becomes very happy; he finds it exciting. He has left his catapult in the Beadon-Street house. There are no squirrels there. Only electric wires, tram and telephone cables. Moti had vicariously fed his desire to hit birds by hitting the cables with stones from his catapult, day after day. The *jhann-jhann* sound of the wires still rings in his ears. As he remembers the city, he looks at Dadu.

""You want to say something?"

Moti smiles ever so slightly.

"You had a big car – a yellow car?"

"Yes," Sarada moves his jaws. "Who did you hear that from?"

"Ma was talking about it one day. Have you sold off the car?"

"What else could I do, bring it with me to the village?" Sarada stops and looks around. "No good roads – what would I do with the car here?"

"That's true." The grandson, too, like the grandfather, turns his head and looks around. Fields, jungle, ponds, ditches and unkempt mud roads – how would Dadu drive here?

"Didn't I do the right thing by selling it off?" Sarada looks into his grandson's eyes. Moti nods his head in assent. Sarada laughs. "Or, would you have me drive my car through the fields to go to the orchards to have mangoes and *jaams*?"

"Of course not," Moti doesn't like the image, either. Besides, plenty of *jaams* and *jaamruls* lie strewn over the grass. Everything would have been smashed to a pulp under the tyres if Dadu had driven his car through the orchard.

Sarada laughs aloud.

"Exactly, my boy. Besides, once they hear the car's horn, all the birds and squirrels of my trees would run away in fear, don't you think so?"

Moti nodded again. Thought about something. Looked this way and that with his elfin eyes. Then ... "I think even the grasshoppers and the butterflies would have run away in fear on hearing the sound of the car."

"That's why the car is a nuisance. No wonder I sold it off," Sarada was pleased with his grandson.

"Except that ..."

"Except what?" Sarada is not ready to budge an inch. "What else can you say about it?" Moti looks downwards and scratches the grass with his toenails. "Unless I get dust on my foot, unless I tread the soft grass underfoot, I wouldn't know that I'm alive." Sarada finished and rubbed his heels vigorously on the grass. That is why, Moti realizes, Dadu is barefoot all day; the Lord of the trees doesn't wear shoes. But Moti begins to feel awkward, not having been able to say the words that had come to the tip of his tongue. Dadu walks. Moti, too, walks with him. The cool shadow of the *jaamrul* orchard slips away from above them. The two of them were now under the sun-baked sky.

"Too hot," Moti said softly.

"This is Jaishtho," Dadu said sharply. "The best month of the best season. Of course it'll be hot – else, how will the mangoes, *jaams*, jackfruits and bananas ripen?"

"That's true, too," Moti mutters his assent. He wipes the sweat off his forehead with the back of his hand. His forehead was sweating the most.

"Here's something you can do." Sarada turns towards his grandson.

"What?" Moti turns towards him.

Sarada stops in his tracks. Moti looks at the old man's eyes. It seems the old man's yellow eyeballs have begun to turn red in the sun.

"The sunshine's hurting your head the most, isn't it?" Sarada smiles softly.

"Yes".

"Of course, it is," Sarada ejects another mass of spit from his throat. The hot, parched sand of the field sucks it dry in the twinkling of an eye. Sarada points to the shorts Moti is wearing. "Take it off; wrap it round your head. Your head will stay cool".

"Oh no! Dadu, you are impossible," giggled Moti. "Shall I walk over the fields naked?"

"I am a cow, a goat; I'm the squirrel on the tree, the fox in the jungle," Sarada made a face and ejected a large mass of spit. "Who's going to see you here? You've become such a big man, h-ah?! Feel embarrassed, huh?" After a pause, Sarada continued, "This is not the dead, stinking sunshine that leaps across the terrace walls of Beadon Street; this is the powerful, direct sunshine that cracks the fields and dries the ponds. Since you are not used to it, it may split your head wide open, too. That is why I say, put it round your head."

As if to please Dadu, Moti takes his shorts off and wraps it round his head. At first, he felt awkward. His ears, cheeks turned red. Then, of course, Moti grew used to it. He began to walk with long strides in step with Dadu. True, who is there to see him in this sun? Not even a crow or magpie in sight. "Understand?" Sarada laughs, puts his hand on his grandson's shoulders. Pleased that his grandson has obeyed him, he says happily, "I don't care about anything. When I'm in the mango orchard or the *jaam* orchard, and I see I'm sweating too much, it's too hot, I take off whatever I have on me and lie down on the grass, spreading my limbs."

"Feels comfortable?"

"Of course it does," Sarada's laugh sounds like the laugh of a little boy. "The soft grass caresses your body, the fragrant shadow of the tree covers your body – how can you help feeling comfortable?"

"No clothes at all?" Moti asked. As if to please Dadu even more, Moti says, "When man used to live in the jungle, they didn't even know what clothes were – that's what I've heard."

"What else? You know all that," Sarada looks up towards the sky. "Man used to be happy in the olden days, now, clothes have added to his discomfort."

Dadu's in a good mood again – Moti realizes this and comes out with what he had wanted to say. "Ma says, your grandfather was such a famous engineer; now he stays in a village like a stupid villager".

"Let her. Let her say it. I don't mind if someone calls me a farmer".

"Ma was rueing the fact that you sold off that big house on Elgin Road."

"Of course, your mother will rue it. She dreams of brick, wood, iron and sand. I dream of soil; I dream of trees."

"Grass, shadows, birds, squirrels," Moti added.

"So, your parents will not know what I have got here in return for a house in the city." Sarada tries to finish off the discussion, as if irritated. "Let them live under the old, stinking sky of the city and dream of palaces; let the smoke and soot of machines and factories gradually shorten their life span." Sarada makes a face and looks at his grandson.

"Will they die before you do, Dadu?" Moti couldn't resist asking. "My mother and father?"

"The whole city of Calcutta is getting ready to die," Dadu laughs through his nose.

Moti seemed to think for a minute. "And the houses? What'll happen to the houses? Those large buildings?" he asked.

"They'll crumble into dust and become one with the soil one day."

"Then?"

"Then, clumps of grass will come up there, trees will come up, flowers will bloom, fruits will appear."

"It'd be so wonderful then, wouldn't it, Dadu? Birds singing, butterflies flitting here and there in Calcutta."

"That's what it'll have to be like. Otherwise, what'll happen to the ever-changing face of the earth?"

Moti came upon a beautiful place, listening to Dadu. He hasn't ever come this way before. A very pretty, round-ish pond. The water shines like a mirror. *Shapla* on one side of the pond, lotus clump on the other. The green lotus leaves float peacefully on the water, round like a *thala*. The *shapla* leaves aren't round; they look somewhat like betel leaves. Two bright-red *shapla* flowers are in bloom. A few more will blossom tomorrow, perhaps a dozen, the day after; many more will blossom the day after that. Numerous buds wait, ready, near the tips of the green stem. A group of grasshoppers fly past the buds, grazing their wings against them. "I don't see lotus buds," Moti was saying. Dadu responded with a laugh, " Not now! You'll have to wait for the monsoon. The rains will bring the buds out; and the flowers will come out in autumn." Moti looked dreamy-eyed at the lotus clump and wondered, when would autumn come, and bunches of lotus flowers bloom? "You're only thinking of flowers on the water? The fish that live in these waters – do you have any idea how big they are? There are carps that are even bigger than you."

Moti forgets the flowers and begins to think of the fish in the water. Big fish – that means fish from a long time back.

"Do old fish taste nice, Dadu?"

The grandson's sudden utterances about eating pleased Dadu. "Do they taste nice, boy?" Sarada's eyes sparkled. "All fresh fish taste nice; I don't care whether new or old."

Moti has realised here that Dadu is crazy about fish.

It's not the one piece of fish or two like they have with rice in Calcutta; Sarada needs lots of fish every mealtime.

Thakuma places bowls full of fried fish, fish curry and fish *charchari* in front of Dadu. That was why Sarada was telling him yesterday, when he sat down to eat, that he had got three ponds dug so that he could eat fish to his heart's content. "Yes, there's a way of eating fish – not just your hand and your mouth; your whole body should smell of fish – that's the way to eat fish."

At that point, Moti remembers his father and his mother. Their washing their hands with soap over and over again lest there remain a whiff of fish-smell on their hands. Ma washes her hands with soap and then puts on powder.

"If you are prone to colds, doctors advise you to have cod liver; they recommend immersion, this medicine and that medicine, you know. I have hot, freshly-fried fish. Coughs and colds don't dare come close."

So, it's only natural that Dadu's eyes will glitter and his tongue dribble with saliva as they talk about fish now. Sarada looks at the water and yawns. "I'm very hungry, my child, I'm absolutely famished."

Moti feigned astonishment, smiled.

"Dadu, you have eaten a lot of mangoes and kheer, then so many *jaams* and *jaamruls*. And already, you're ..."

"Mine is not a stomach; it's a barrel. Doesn't ever want to get filled – aren't you hungry?" Sarada turned towards Moti.

Moti shook his head.

"Not even a bit."

"Yours, too, is not a stomach; it's a homoeopathic phial."

Moti laughed out aloud at his grandfather's words. Sarada doesn't spit this time; he swallows a large gulp.

"The sun's right over our head, see?" he says and looks up at the sky. "Today, the fishermen have cast their nets in the northern pond. By now, the fish has reached the house, I'm sure. Hmmmm! *Chital*, I've told them. I think your Thakuma has got down to cooking *kalia* with the *chital* middles."

"Possibly," Moti giggled. "That is why you are raving hungry."

"What do you mean, 'possibly'?" Sarada bursts out. "I'm sure the old lady is cooking *kalia*. I can smell it from here."

Old man, or a small child? – he's so greedy and mischievous. He has to be like that, Moti reasons. If one is to extend one's life span at this age, one has to act like a young man, the old bat has to climb to the top of the tree and eat *jaam* and *jaamrul*, get bowled over by the thought of fish *kalia*.

"So, you're returning home now, Dadu?" the grandson asks.

"Of course. I don't feel like doing anything else or going anywhere else when I think of eating."

"But, I still haven't seen the pineapple orchard", mischievously, Moti said, "I wanted to roam some more with you, see your guava orchard."

"The guavas are stone-hard now. Wait for *Aashar.* Let a few showers wet them – only then will the guavas ripen. Now, even bats don't touch guavas."

So, Moti desists.

Sarada loosens the *gamchha* full of *jaams* and *jaamruls* from his waist. "Here, hold this. We'll have some for your Thakuma. The old lady doesn't have a single fruit unless they have been plucked by me."

Moti reaches out and takes the bunch of fruits.

"You, too, can eat a few if you want. There's enough. Here, sit down in the shade and eat." Sarada is busy taking off the belt tied round his waist.

Yes, Moti will eat a fruit or two if he feels like it. The shade at the side of the pond is wonderful. A huge *horitaki* tree towers over him. A dense cane bush all around the pond. But, what is his grandfather doing?

"Dadu, what are you ...?" Moti stops.

"Yes," Sarada yanks his belt off in one motion. "I'll take a dip right here. I won't get the chance to bathe at home. I'll go and sit down to eat at once. Fish *kalia* and rice." Sarada laughed.

Moti was afraid or was he startled? He felt his heart in his mouth. He quickly looks the other way.

Leaving his shorts on the grass, Dadu went down to the river. If this had been their Maniktolla crossing or Sealdah – many men, many shops, cars, policemen, vendors – then, Moti would have thought the man was mad. Once. Moti had spied such an old madman from the tram on his way to his *mashi*'s house. Totally naked; the people on the road were laughing at him. But, now? Here?

Moti turned around. Gulped. Looked fearfully at the shorts Sarada had taken off on the grass. Then he seemed to become bolder. He looked up and watched the water. Dadu is swimming. As Moti's eyes met his grandfather's, Dadu laughed and disappeared into the water. The man cannot be seen any more. One, two, three – Moti tries to count – how long can Dadu stay underwater? The lotus leaves shiver in the distance, as the water laps up to them; the *shapla* stems sway in the current along with their buds. Moti understood Dadu is swimming underwater to some point far away. And just then, the *horitoki* leaves above him rustled in the wind. A *dahuk* cries in the distance – to which side of the cane bush is it? A white cloud has floated in from nowhere and lies suspended in a corner of the sky – a kingfisher dives into the water and immediately flies off with a silvery something in its beak.

Moti is enjoying all this. He takes out a *kalojaam* from his bundle and pops it into his mouth. Yes, Dadu is taking *jaam* for Thakuma. He thinks of Baba. Ma. Baba never has *jaam*, *jaamruul*, mangoes or pineapples with him when he returns home from office; he brings Ma's powder, snow and cream. Moti lets out a short sigh and then gets up. Moti suddenly realizes he, too, is naked. He had listened to Dadu and had taken his shorts off to cover his head; he hasn't put it on after that. Still, he wasn't feeling at all like putting it on. His father had bought it for him from College Street. No matter, no need for it; it's unnecessary, he thought. He really wanted to get into the pond in this state, just like his grandfather. To swim underwater and reach the *shapla* and the lotus clumps. But, it doesn't matter what he wishes, for he cannot swim.

Still, he tried not to feel sad. Some bird had settled on a *horitoki* branch and was chirping away. Dadu's head floats up over the water. He dives in again. Dadu is diving in and meeting the old fish under the water, Moti thinks. He is so fond of fish – who knows, he may even catch a fish with his bare hands and drag it ashore.

Thinking along those lines, Moti is about to reach his hand into Thakuma's bundle of *jaam*s and take out one when he suddenly stops, astonished. The jingle of laughter. Somebody is laughing behind him. Moti stands straight. Turns around. A girl. Standing near the cane bushes. A branch of cane fruits in her hand. She is devouring the fruits and staring at Moti. Her eyes glint. Tall, slim figure. Moti has discovered the black *basak* tree after coming here. The slim, tall girl reminded him of the thin and frail *basak* stem. The same black complexion. She sways with the rhythm of laughter, just as the *basak* stem dances in the wind, shivers to its touch.

But, as Moti saw the way the girl was staring at him, his ears blushed and grew hot. He is a clever boy, a city boy. It does not take him a second to understand the meaning of her glance – he snatched his shorts from the grass and put it on. Already, he is sweating profusely.

"What do you want? What are you staring at?" Moti puts on his shorts, stands up straight and shouts at her.

"Nothing. I'm just having a cane fruit," Moti gnashes his teeth in anger. He stares at the girl. The saree she has on is as black as she is. And, torn, at that. But her teeth are pearl-white. Moti likes her teeth, sparkling white as the wings of the crane. Likes them, but he suddenly remembers something, and feels his heart miss a beat. He looked at the cast-off large shorts on the grass out of the corner of his eye. He knows what state Dadu is in now, swimming under the water. Dadu seems to have finished his bath; isn't that him swimming towards the shore?

"Hey! Where do you think you're going?" Moti barks out, even louder than before. "Where are you going?"

"I'll have some water." She has a jute sack with her. Moti hadn't noticed it before. The girl drags the sack from the cane bushes and places it beside the *horitoki* tree, then, she steps out as if to go towards the pond to drink.

"No! You don't have to drink now," Moti confronts her. "What do you have in that sack?"

"Dry leaves."

"Oh! So you are a scavenger." Moti bends down and inspects the contents of the sack. Dry leaves and a couple of pineapples, cut quite recently from the garden. Moti stands erect.

"Where did you get the pineapples?"

The girl falters initially, then smiles and points at the pond.

"From Rajababu's fields. I cut two down to eat with salt."

That means they're from Dadu's orchard. She had pointed to the pond and had called Dadu Rajababu, Moti understood.

"Rajababu will flay you. You've cut the young, unripe pineapples."

"Won't say anything to me. I eat so many fruits from Rajababu's trees, his orchards, he doesn't say anything." The girl displays her white teeth, as white as the wings of the crane, and laughs, shakes her head and raises her eyebrows. Then ... "Let me go and quench my thirst with the sweet water of Rajababu's pond." So saying, she made a sudden twist with her hips and walked quickly over the grass towards the pond. Moti stands and stares. The fear that had assailed him a short while ago began to haunt him again. The girl has gone right up to the edge of the water. Dadu hasn't moved from the deep water to the waist-high water. Yeesh! Moti bit his lip. His face became pale as ash. Then, would Dadu climb ashore like that in front of that big girl? Dadu! He wanted to yell, and warn the old man – but no sound comes out of his throat. Fear, astonishment, disgust, anticipation. Aversion, sadness and many other small and large currents played through his heart. All, in those few moments. Not a madman, not a child, Moti said to himself, my grandfather, Sarad Ray, one-time famous engineer, resident of Elgin Road, has been transformed into an animal, a demon, a fearful, ugly beast.

Is she laughing? Is the girl laughing at Dadu? But Dadu is

still in waist-high water Even his navel cannot be seen. Moti focussed his gaze like a microscope on the pond and gulped. The top of the horitoki tree above him began to rustle in the wind again. The *dahuk* calls afar, in the cane bush. The white cloudy mass in one corner of the sky has become even whiter and is being torn apart like cotton-wool. But Moti was not enjoying any of this. His eyes, his mind, his entire attention is now at the edge of the water and in the water.

What's that – Dadu's smiling at the girl, nodding at her? The girl has dipped her feet into the water and has sat down on the steps of the ghat. Isn't that Dadu's grey-white hairy belly rising above the water? Wasn't that his navel he just saw? Moti shivers. He cannot breathe, cannot gulp. But, almost right then, Moti managed to breathe out softly and gulp voraciously. Dadu has again moved to neck-high water, the water meant for swimming in. Dadu is swimming. The girl raises her hands and points to the *shapla* forests. Sarada tears off the large *shapla* flower alongwith its green stem and dives again. Then he surfaces again on this side of the pond. Moti's heart begins to beat faster again. But, no – this time, Sarada doesn't step on the stairs of the ghat and come up to the waist-high or chest-high water like before. The water is near his neck. Sarada's jaw above the water. He throws the red *shapla* flower along with its stem towards land. The girl reaches out her hand and catches it. Then she tears the flower off from the stem and pushes it into her bun. Dadu stands in neck-high water and smiles. The girl smiles, too. After she has finished putting the flower into her bun, the girl bends down and scoops up palmfuls of water and drinks. The red flower in her hair was trembling in the wind. After drinking, she stands up straight. Then she climbs to the green grass on the shore and the trunk of the horitoki tree in one swift motion. She lifts the sack of dry leaves onto her shoulders. Then, she raises a swift twist with her waist and enters the cane bush on the other side. As if her way out is through the cane bush.

Moti stares at that direction for some time and feels reassured; he heaves a sigh of relief. Good, the trouble-maker is gone, he muttered, and immediately turned his gaze towards the pond to see Dadu. "Have you finished your bath, Dadu?" Moti called out in a cheerful voice. He could, now.

"Yes, my child, I'm done. I'm almost done".Sarada leaves the water and emerges onto dry land. The *dahuk* is crying very loud. The white, thin clouds now merged into each other like strands of cotton-wool and began to take the form of a massive, white lotus. A wonderful cloud-flower. A happy Moti was looking at Dadu. Water drips from his ears, the tip of his nose, his jaws, from his fingers. Dadu's naked body reminded Moti of an old tree. A tree that has come up on land after spending ages under the water. The Lord of the trees must be a tree, after all, Moti thought. The grey-white hair on Dadu's body was like moss on the tree's trunk. Water drips drop by drop from the moss. Moti listens carefully to the rustle of the *horitoki* tree.

Sarada puts on his shorts. Tightens the belt with a vengeance.

Moti picks up the bundle of *jaams* for Thakuma.

"I took a bit of extra time, didn't I, grandson?"

Moti smiles, doesn't utter a word. He walks with Dadu.

"The water of my pond is beautifully cold. Once you dive in, you just don't feel like coming out." "Hunnh," Moti makes an incoherent sound at first. Then he muses over something and says, "I think Thakuma must have finished cooking the kalia a long time ago and must be waiting for you."

Sarada doesn't say anything; he keeps walking. Moti, too, walks silently. Is Dadu thinking of something? Moti wonders. A red grasshopper walks in front of Dadu; it flutters near his head, his forehead.

"Dadu?"

"What is it?" Sarada doesn't spit; he looks at his grandson out of the corner of his eye. His grandson walks with him, hand in hand with him. "The girl has cut two pineapples from your orchard; she's hidden it between the dry leaves."

"Hmmmm," Sarada laughs softly. "She'll eat the unripe pineapple with salt and chillies, I think." Sarada notices the red grasshopper in front of his forehead. "Let her. How much will she eat? There are more than a thousand pineapples in my fields at this time."

Moti breathed out softly.

Sarada now walks with his hand on his grandson's shoulder.

"Bats, squirrels, magpies, bulbulis – they waste a lot of my fruits. Let them. I don't mind at all. I have lots; that's why they eat."

Moti is silent. He has walked a lot and his feet have gone dead. But he suddenly discovers something and seems to become animated and excited. Dadu's hand rests on his shoulder. The smell of Dadu's body, his smell wafts up his nostrils. Not the smell of fish, not the smell of mangoes, not the smell of kheer, not the smell of *jaamrul*. Is it the smell of water? Of the moss? No, not that either. It is the soft, sweet, cool smell of the *shapla* flower. Moti didn't understand if it was necessary to hold on to this smell with one's body in order to extend one's life span. Unable to understand, he began to feel a restlessness gnaw away inside him. And continued to walk.

Originally published in Bangla as *Boner Raja*.

CUSTOMS DUTY

Narendranath Mitra

Translated By Sayantan Dasgupta

Dhaka Mail will leave at ten p.m., but Lalmohan Saha arrives at the station some two hours in advance. He has with him a large trunk, two suitcases, a basket of food and his bedding. With the help of the coolie, Lalmohanbabu got his luggage down from the rickshaw. Then, after telling the coolie to come back at the right time, he lit a beedi. Of course, he had bought his ticket in advance, but, these days, having a ticket doesn't guarantee that you will be able to board the train smoothly with your luggage. One has to get the approval of Land Customs; there, every bag and trunk is opened and checked. They search every piece of baggage to see if the passenger is taking any contraband goods to Pakistan. No leniency, absolutely none. Lalmohan has suffered a reverse some fifteen days ago. The Customs officer had confiscated fifteen yards of printed fabric and five mill sarees from his suitcase. Lalmohan had prayed and pleaded, he had thrown himself at the officer's feet; he had even tried to push a couple of rupees into the officer's left hand. But his attempts had backfired; the officer had got mad and had wanted to hand him over to the police. He had managed to evade imprisonment only after a lot of sweat. That's the end of this business for me, he had told himself. But he'd forgotten his vow as soon as he returned to Calcutta. If you are in business, you have to take both losses and gains in your stride. You have to take various kinds of risks. Merchants lose so many thousands of rupees, but do they stop doing business and sit idle because of that? Of course, Lalmohan is not a merchant; it's difficult for him to meet a loss of a hundred-odd rupees, let alone thousands and lakhs. Still, Lalmohan couldn't just sit idle, twiddling his fingers. This is the most flourishing business in Pakistan. Three hundred-four hundred per cent profit. Many traders, big and small, are carrying on with their business under the same circumstances. This time, too, when he came to Calcutta, Lalmohan went and invested some three hundred rupees in sarees, dhotis and printed fabric. Stuffed the material into bags and beddings. Some bags have fruit near the top, others have vegetables, innocent, inconsequential trifles like that. But, this time, Lalmohan is forewarned; he has been trying to find a solution to his problem. He won't go to the male Customs Officer this time. He will have to take the help of a woman and get his stuff passed by a lady Customs Officer. Lalmohan has been doing the rounds here for the last few days and has observed that the department has a few young women from decent families. They let the baggage of women passengers pass with only a cursory look; they don't meddle much with the contents. The women's counter is the easiest and the most comfortable way out. This is the route Lalmohan will take to get his stuff passed.

True, he doesn't have any woman with him. There's his old mother at home, and his widowed elder sister, who has become a burden on his shoulders with her three kids. Lalmohan throws them out of his house thrice a day, saying, "Times are bad; it won't be possible for me to feed anybody else. Go and fend for yourselves." Later, he pulls his sister and her children back home from the banyan tree or the river ghat. From where will he arrange for a woman here in Calcutta? But, even if he cannot bring a woman here, there are others who do. For instance, Harabilas Sil has brought his family here to get his wife treated for a woman's disease. Harabilas's wife's treatment is over. She'd had to stay in hospital for only a week or so. Lalmohan visited her thrice during those seven days and bought her *bedanas* and oranges. "Remember, Hara*da*, we'll go back together," he had said with a smile on his face. "Of course, we will," Harabilas had answered.

"I'll have some baggage with me, *Boudi,*" Lalmohan had said, looking at Sunayoni, Harabilas's wife. "You'll have to say

I'm your own brother-in-law if they ask." "Of course, I'll tell them. You *are* our own – are you an outsider, or what? But, you'll have to sell me a pretty saree cheap, my dear," Sunayoni had said, smiling.

"Oh! You don't worry about that, *Boudi,*" Lalmohan had said. "Just you get well. Don't worry about the saree."

All the details have been finalised. Harabilas, too, will leave today, accompanied by his wife. And with them will go Lalmohan, masquerading as Lakshman, the brother-in-law. All his stuff is inside Harabilas's wife, Sunayoni's baggage.

Lalmohan has tied up all the loose ends. No more worries. Lalmohan sat on the large trunk and began to puff away at his beedi. He began to look around every now and then – if only Harabilas turns up with his wife now. Not only is Harabilas Sil from his village, but he lives in his *paara*, his neighbourhood, as well. Lalmohan shares a cordial relationship with him. Harabilas is a very clever and crafty man. And Lalmohan's biggest reassurance? He has his wife with him.

Rickshaws, taxis and horse-carts crowded into the station. So many men walked in with women of varying age. But strangely, there is no sign of Harabilas! Impatient, Lalmohan has got up from the trunk and is about to step forward to look for them when a young man of twenty two or twenty three walks up to him. "Here you are, Malu*da*, there's no end to the number of places I've looked for you."

Haripada is Harabilas's cousin, his father's sister's son. It's at his house in Ultadanga that Harabilas has been staying.

"Where are your *Dada* and *Boudi*?" Lalmohan asked.

"That's what I've come to tell you," Haripada said. "*Dada* won't be able to go. *Boudi*'s condition has worsened. The doctor has said there's no question of moving her for the next two-three weeks, let alone days."

After Haripada had gone. Lalmohan just sat there for some time, cradling his head in his arms. No, he'll get on the train this very day, be it by hook or by crook. He cannot wait. It has cost him one-and-a-half rupees to bring the luggage here by rickshaw. He'll have to pay another one-and-a-half rupees to have it hauled back. Besides, how long can he afford to pay his hotel bill in Calcutta? How much money does he have with him, anyway?

In terms of presence of mind, Lalmohan is Harabilas's equal. So what if Harabilas and his wife are not going today; there are many other passengers on Dhaka Mail, who are travelling with their wives. He just needs to meet up with them.

A nattily-dressed handsome young man was walking towards the women's section of Land Customs with his luggage and his beautiful wife. Lalmohan went directly up to him and said, "Just a minute, sir. Where is your home?"

"Faridpur," said the astonished young man. "But, why do you ask?"

"I am from Faridpur, too," said Lalmohan. "We're from the same district then. Can you do me a favour, brother?"

"Tell me how I can help."

Lalmohan pointed to his luggage and said, "Not much, actually. Boudi will just get this stuff passed along with her things. She'll just have to say that I am with you and that this luggage, too, is yours."

Abani raised his brows, looked at Lalmohan for some time, smiled and said, "Well, I don't think my wife will mind introducing you as our man, but we have some problems with your luggage. Things have got very strict these days, you know. They literally rifle through everything."

Lalmohan looked up another four or five men who were travelling with their wives and made the same request to them. But they all said almost the same thing. In these times of harsh rigidity, who will knowingly take such a risk?

Lalmohan was disappointed, but not defeated. He has always been a stubborn person. Once he has got an idea into his head, it's difficult to dissuade him. Not only does he begin spewing invectives when he gets angry, he also begins to formulate new plans and strategies.

"Let's see what rail company can stop me today," Lalmohan told his companion, Nanda Das. "Ok, you sit here for some time. Look after this stuff. I'll go and take a look at the men's section of Customs."

Nanda Das, who is Lalmohan's neighbour, is also travelling with him. Of the prohibited stuff, only a seer of *atta* is his. He'll say, "This is my *ekadashi* dinner." If they still refuse to pass it, he'll just have to leave it behind; Nanda's one of the meek, submissive ones. It is not his will to be involved in all this, but Lalmohan's will is more powerful than his.

"Let me push off today. You can always go when it suits you, tomorrow."

"Oh! Shut up!" Lalmohan rebuked him. "Do what I say. Take care of the stuff. I'll go today, and so will you. If I fail to go, I won't let you go, either."

Making Nanda sit down with the luggage, Lalmohan set out to reconnoitre the Customs counter for male passengers and to find out how crowded it was today and how strict the checking was. On the way, he kept darting his eyes here and there, looking for men who were accompanied by women.

He crossed the crowds of destitute refugees on the right. They have well and truly made their home at the edge of the station. Somebody eats, somebody sleeps, husband and wife quarrel, romance, too, goes on side by side – Lalmohan walks on, looking at them. Regardless of what people may say, we are much better off in Pakistan than these people, thought Lalmohan.

"Babu, wait."

Hearing a feminine voice behind him, Lalmohan turned back and looked. He stopped in his tracks, startled. A girl, around eighteen or nineteen, in a tattered saree. So much dirt on her body that her original complexion cannot be deciphered. Short. Despite all this, though, there's a certain grace to her body. Joint eyebrows, well-delineated nose and eyes, long hair. Lalmohan remembered, he had seen this girl quarrelling with a sickly old woman a short while back. Lalmohan looked at the girl for a while and then asked, "What is it?"

The girl hesitated a bit and said, "The whole day, today, I haven't had a single morsel. My frail mother, she's fasting, too. She'd gulp me down if she could – she's so hungry. Please, give me something, no?"

She has only a bunch of blue glass bangles round her arm, Lalmohan notices. Doesn't look bad on her at all. A nice, shapely hand. Nice, tall fingers, their ends, narrow.

"I don't have the time to be merciful, nor the money," Lalmohan said roughly. He turned his face away quickly. But the girl called again from behind him, "Please ... Give me something before you go." Lalmohan gave her another look. No, not a bad specimen at all. Would pass as someone from a decent family.

"I can, but you'll have to do as I say," Lalmohan said.

The girl looked into his eyes. It's not as if she doesn't know what she will have to do. She has had to do what one or two others have said before. When they hear her speak of her belly-hunger, a different kind of hunger blazes in their eyes – it's not as if she is oblivious to that fact.

The girl takes a few more steps forward, smiles lightly, lowers her voice, and says, "Of course, I will. Tell me what I have to do, and I'll do it. What is it?"

"I can't tell you here – come with me," Lalmohan said. "What's your name?

"Champa".

Lalmohan said sweetly, "Nice name. Come, my girl, come."

Lalmohan walked a short distance to the first-class waiting room, pushed the door open, and peeped in. Not a man in sight. "Come on," Lalmohan said as he looked back at the girl again.

Champa followed him in.

Lalmohan went and stood a little closer to her. Champa took a step backwards and said, "First tell me what you'll give me."

Lalmohan didn't touch any part of her body; he only took his mouth close to hers and said, "If you help me with something, I'll give you anything you want."

Then, Lalmohan whispered some more and explained to Champa the nature of the job.

A strange proposal! A few others like Lalmohan have previously called her to talk to her. They have spoken their hearts, too. But, nobody has said anything like this.

Champa hesitated, thought about it, and said, "But, what if they catch me?"

Lalmohan smiled. "You know what'll happen then. We'll have to go to jail, hand in hand. I hear, it's not a bad place. Food comes free, so does lodging."

"Okay, It's all right with me," said Champa. "But they'll catch me out right at the beginning. Your fresh, washed, white clothes, and my dirty, torn saree. Why should they take us as husband and wife?"

A pleased Lalmohan said, "Right, you are. You have brains, Champa. If you keep your wits about you, you can be wed to a judge or a magistrate, forget about me. Wait a bit. I'll go and make the arrangements."

Within minutes, Lalmohan returned, the small tin suitcase in his hand. Below his cast-off worn clothes, a small mirror and a mini comb, two bundles of beedis and matchboxes and other such knick-knacks were different kinds of different-coloured sarees. Lalmohan brought out a wide-bordered champa-coloured saree from the bundle. "Here, put this on. I don't think we'll look ill-matched now. They cost seventeen rupees and fourteen annas. I'll sell them at thirty rupees a piece, at least – I may get more – at the Munsi's house when I get back."

"You'll just sell, won't you give your wife one?" Champa said.

"Wife? Where's the wife?" laughed Lalmohan. "You're my wife, remember?"

An embarrassed Champa lowered her glance. Then, she looked at Lalmohan again out of the corner of her eye. Fair, beautiful, slim figure. Lalmohan is quite a handsome, young man. He can't be more than twenty five or twenty six.

"Okay, now go and stand outside," said Champa.

"Why?"

Champa smiled to herself. It's true – he is a bachelor. He doesn't understand anything about women.

"Still asks 'why'. Don't I have to change my clothes?" Champa responded, raising her eyebrows.

"Oh!" said Lalmohan, flustered. "And yes, it won't just do to put on an expensive saree. You're travelling with your husband, a married woman. You'll need *sindoor* (vermillion) on your parting and forehead. You put on the saree; I'll get you the *sindoor*. I'll buy a platform ticket as well."

Lalmohan returned some time later. Not just *sindoor*, he has also brought a couple of sweet *paan*s. He proffered one *paan* towards Champa and said, "Have it, yes. Have it and dye your lips red. A housewife, a married woman, after all. Doesn't look right unless you have *paan*."

"All right, that, I'll have. But, an unmarried woman, me – how long can I keep the *sindoor* on? People will notice."

The station clock made a *dhong* sound. And Lalmohan jumped up immediately. "Yeeeesh! It's 9:30. Whatever decking up you have to do, get it done; won't be able to catch the train after this."

After a couple of minutes, Champa said, "Come, I'm done."

Lalmohan gave her a once-over. The yellow saree has suited Champa well. She has worn it rather nicely, too, taut, coiled around her. Sindoor on her parting, a nice, round drop on her forehead. Will pass easily as the housewife of a decent, well-to-do family.

Lalmohan said, "Raise the veil a bit more. These days, nobody uses such a long ghomta. And the hair hasn't been combed properly. It's still tousled; they may suspect. Let me hold the mirror up; you run the comb through your hair some more."

She hasn't oiled her head recently. How can she comb her hair properly? Instead of mentioning the oil, Champa said, "This'll have to do."

Lalmohan's skepticism knows no end. He held out the mirror in front to Champa, then, after a slight hesitation, he himself ran the comb through her hair once or twice, and said, "It's okay, now."

Champa looks at her newly-wed *sindoor*-on-the-parting image in the mirror, was quiet for a while, and then said, "Come, let's go, then."

"Another thing," Lalmohan said. "It won't do to address me so formally, in the honorific. Address me more informally, we are husband and wife. Very special to each other. Do remember that, understand?"

Lalmohan creased his face with a smile.

Champa, too, smiled a shy smile. "Understood. Let's go now."

Nanda Das is fidgeting restlessly on the trunk there. He saw Lalmohan and said, "You go with the suitcase, and you're gone. You plan to go today or not?" But he spots Champa behind Lalmohan and stops. Asks in wonder, "Who the hell is that?"

"My wife," said Lalmohan.

"Wife!" Nanda repeated, astonished.

"Yes, yes, my family," said Lalmohan. "And you're my brother-in-law, my wife's brother. You've come to see me off. Here, take your platform ticket. And you've already bought the train ticket. Give me the ticket, let's see."

Nanda hesitates. Lalmohan berated him. "Ah! Delaying again! If you want to go home, do as I say, I tell you."

Lalmohan helped the luggage onto the coolie's head and went and stood in the queue for women passengers at Customs with Nanda and Champa. The queue is not too long. A good-looking girl of twenty two or twenty three is opening the luggage of the women passengers and searching them. Gold bangles on her left hand, and a wrist watch too. Glasses perched on her nose, a sweet face.

"Go! Move up to the front," Lalmohan told Champa as he nudged her forward. "Show her what you are carrying."

Champa looked back at Lalmohan and then walked up to the front.

The lady Customs Officer looked at her once, then gave their luggage a once-over, and said, "Two tickets and so much luggage. How many in all? These four, right?"

"Oh, yes, these four."

"You're not hiding any contraband stuff in there, planning to take it across, are you?"

Champa smiled a little. "Why don't you open it and check?"

The lady Customs Officer is not one to give up. "That, I will have to. Take the lock off. Where's the key?"

Champa and Lalmohan felt their hearts beat faster. Who knows what will happen now? They're done for, if she is thorough with it.

Lalmohan took the key out of his pocket, handed it to Champa and said, "See, I told you. Open up now. I told you then not to bring such a huge trunk. You'll have to come back again, anyway. You and your mother, you're made for each other."

Then Lalmohan looked at the lady Customs Officer and said in the Calcutta dialect, "She won't leave a single thing behind, understand? And mother-in-law doesn't have any sense, either. She's filled up the trunk with loads of old kanthas, clothes and pickle jars as if she's the only woman whose daughter is expecting."

It was not just Champa, the lady officer, too, blushed. Drops of sweat appeared on the lady officer's forehead. She wiped her face with a small handkerchief, or was she trying to hide the hint of a smile, who knows?

Lalmohan looked at Champa disgustedly and said, "Move! Let me go through! I will open them myself. What was the need for you to travel in this condition; why couldn't you have stayed on at your father's place for a few days? Can one cope with the hassles of travel in this condition, you tell me? The trip from home to here, and she's already turned pale, see.

Lalmohan looked at the lady Customs Officer and said, "She still has to spend the whole night on the train."

"That's all right, that's all right," said the lady. "You don't need to open that one. Let me see the others."

Then she raised the lids of the two suitcases and glanced at the contents, prodded the bedding with her soft finger. "Okay, you can pass."

The three of them waded through the sea of passengers and soon found themselves standing in front of platform number six. The checker hardly glanced at the tickets. Nodded his permission for them to go inside. The coolie has the baggage on his head. Lalmohan carries the suitcase. "Oh, no! Look how crowded the train is," Lalmohan said, looking at Nanda. "Hope we can get inside. Go to the front with the coolie. Check if the crowd's a little less in the compartment behind the engine. I'll say my goodbyes to her."

A goods train stands, motionless, towards the north. "This way! Hurry up and come this way," Lalmohan said as he walked that way. "Shit! It's almost time. Hope I'll be able to board the train, after all. Okay, go behind the goods train, take the saree off, fold it and bring it to me. And, yes, how much should I pay you, how much do you want?"

Lalmohan is very busy, very tense. It's almost time for the train to move, but the luggage is still with the coolie.

"How much do you want? Out with it," said Lalmohan.

Champa was silent for a moment. She stared, round-eyed at Lalmohan. Then she said, "You said you'd give me whatever I wanted."

"Yes, I did say so. How much do you want? What do you want?"

"What can I say? You give me what your heart tells you to," said Champa.

Lalmohan mulled about something, then he counted out a rupee in quarters-annas-two annas from his pocket and handed the change to Champa. "Here, I've given you a whole rupee. Don't complain, now. If only I can manage to get aboard with the luggage."

Without replying to this, Champa stood behind the train and took off the beautiful saree. Then she folded it carefully and handed it over to Lalmohan.

Lalmohan gave Champa the platform ticket and said, "Show them this at the gate. The checker will let you through. And, have you counted? Sixteen annas?"

Champa looked at Lalmohan's face again. She seemed to laugh ever so slightly. "Yes. All of sixteen annas," she said.

Lalmohan didn't wait any longer. He turned around and marched towards the train. There might just be some space in the car behind the engine. Nanda's an imbecile. A worthless fellow. You could never depend on him to do something properly.

But he found Nanda had got the luggage onto the train with the help of the coolie. The train's much less crowded than it is on other days. Nanda's even managed to make himself space to sit. He saw Lalmohan and cried out to him, "Hurry up! I've held on to some space for you. The coolie wouldn't settle for anything less than a rupee and a half."

Lalmohan glanced at the luggage, wriggled into the tiny space beside Nanda and heaved a sigh of relief. Then he took out two cigarettes from his pocket, offered Nanda one and said, "Light up! Oof! I wasn't sure I could manage it today."

The last bell sounded.

What a coincidence! The handsome young man – the first one he had spoken to – he sits opposite them, and he, too, has lit a cigarette. His decked-up wife sits beside him.

"So, *Dada*, you're on this train, too?" said Lalmohan.

"You managed it in the end?! How did you?" asked Abani, smiling.

Lalmohan smiled mysteriously. "Managed it. You didn't help me, left me by the roadside"

An embarrassed Abani said, "Oh, no. Never. But how did you manage it at the last minute with all your luggage? Who did you come with?"

Lalmohan smiled softly. "With my wife, who else?"

"What's that? Your wife? You have a wife, is it?" Abani said, astonished.

"Why shouldn't I? Are you the only married man in the world, *Dada*? Is there nobody else?"

Sushma, Abani's wife, now smitten by curiosity, looked at him with a faint smile on her lips. Pretty face, and that beautiful, round drop of *sindoor* on her forehead.

Lalmohan felt his heart race. There was a drop just like this on Champa's forehead. It had made her look just as beautiful.

"No, no, that's not what I meant," Abani said, feeling awkward. "So, your wife..."

Lalmohan didn't hear the rest. He didn't want to. He averted his eyes and looked outside. The train has started to move. But Lalmohan is well used to jumping onto and from such slow-moving trains. He can still get down from the train if he wishes to. He can still run up to her and clutch her hand.

But whose hand will Lalmohan go and clutch? Can he find Champa again in the crowd? Can she be recognised again? Insulted, hurt, has she not wiped it off already? Or, has she, smitten by the hurt, made the *sindoor* her asset; is she using it, at this very moment, to pass somebody else's stuff, posing as his companion?

Grains of unburnt coal kept getting into Lalmohan's eyes.

The train runs on at full gallop.

Originally published in Bangla as *Shulko*.

BHARATVARSHA

Ramapada Chowdhury

Translated By Sayantan Dasgupta

BF Three Thirty-two, it was called in military parlance. It was really not a station at all; it neither had a platform, nor a ticket counter. One just woke up one morning to find that a fence of shiny, new barbed wire had come up beside the lines. That was all. Not a single train used to stop there the whole day. Actually, one did stop – a special train. One fine morning, it would suddenly come and draw up at the station. Only we got to know beforehand on which day and at what time it would arrive – the five of us, if you count Bhagwatilal, the Bihari cook.

No station, no train stopped there, yet a new name had gained currency among the railway people. Andahalt. 'Anda', meaning egg. At the foot of the two midget hills bordering Andahalt lay a Mahato village – chicken strutted around freely there. The Mahatos would travel far, far away to the *haat*s of Bhoorkunda to sell their fowl and eggs. Sometimes, they would go cockfighting with their precious cocks tucked in their armpits. But all that did not lead to BF Three Thirty-two getting to be called Andahalt.

Honestly, the eggs of the Mahato village held no charm for us.

The Railways had an arrangement with our man. He had a manually operated trolley, too. Sporting a red piece of cloth, it used to come rolling over the rails to reach the stuff. It used to bring us loads and loads of eggs. Bhagwatilal, the Bihari cook, would boil them the night before. But that did not lead to the name Andahalt, either. The name owed its origin to the shells of full-boiled eggs that were gradually accumulating in a heap on that side of the barbed-wire fence, to the shells that were turning into a mountain day by day.

The first two letters of the BF-32 of military parlance was not some code, but rather an abbreviation of the word, 'breakfast', we reckoned.

There was a POW camp in Ramgarh at that time; Italian prisoners of war were kept there, fenced in by bayonets and barbed wire. Once in a while, they used to be herded on to a train and sent off somewhere along this way. Why and where, none of us knew.

We would only get the news that a train came and stopped here early next morning. We would read our man's letter the previous day and pointing to the basket of eggs, tell our cook, Bhagwatilal, "*Teensau tees* breakfast."

Bhagwatilal would count out six-hundred-and-sixty and another twenty-five as extras, just in case some turned out to be rotten. Then he would boil them in water till they became brick-hard and set about helping the three-server coolies to take the shells off.

That was what kept piling up day by day beyond the barbed wire. The train would arrive early in the morning and military guards would immediately hop down from either side of the train. They would guard the prisoners of war, their rifles poised by their side. The foreign prisoners clad in their striped uniforms would climb down one by one from the train with a large-ish mug and enamel plate in their hands.

The three-server coolies would position themselves after placing two large drums upside down to make them serve as tables, and the visitors would stand in queue to walk up one by one to get their breakfast. One coolie would pour the coffee into the mug, another would hand out two slices of bread to each, and the third would hand each of them a pair of eggs. Then they would climb back onto the train. I-E on his shoulder; the guard in the khaki bush shirt would blow his whistle and wave his flag and the train would depart.

The Mahatos would never come close; they would take a break from sowing their *jonar* seeds, straighten up in their fields and stare, wide eyed.

Sometimes, after the train had left, we would entrust the tent to Bhagwatilal's care and make our way towards the Mahato village in search of vegetables. In the rocky soil of the hilly slopes, they used to raise mustard crops, brinjal and *jhinga* too.

Then, one day, Andahalt turned into a halt station overnight. *Moorum*, the red-brick dust, was brought in and strewn to raise the fenced-in area near the lines to resemble a platform. From that time on, it wasn't just the POWs, military specials too, would come and stop there once in a while. Gaberdine pants-clad, purse-tucked-into-hip-pocket American military special. The military police would get down from the train and stroll around, even make a jest or two, and the group of soldiers would, as always, queue up, mug and *thala* in hand, and one by one, get their bread and their eggs and have their mugs filled with coffee. Then they would climb into their respective cars; the guard in the khaki bush shirt would blow his whistle and wave his flag, and I would run and get the supply form okayed by the Major. The train would leave; in which direction, towards what destination, none of us would know.

On that day too, a train of American soldiers had screeched to a halt at the station. The three server-coolies were serving eggs and bread and coffee. Bhagwatilal was keeping a watch to see if anyone would throw a tantrum about 'rotten' eggs and bread. When things were going thus my eyes suddenly fell on the other side of the barbed wire fence.

Some distance away from the fence, a Mahato boy in loincloth stood and stared, wide-eyed. I had once seen this boy with his iron charm strung across his *ghunshi*, the thread on his waist, riding on the back of a bullock.

The boy was looking at the train with awe in his eyes, or perhaps, he was watching the rosy-cheeked American soldiers. A soldier spied him and let out a sudden loud "Hey", and immediately the boy in loincloth ran off helter-skelter towards the Mahato village. A few American soldiers had a good laugh over it. I thought the boy would never come back again.

None of the Mahatos would ever come there, not a single one of them. They would just straighten up from their work in the field and stare from afar with wonder in their eyes.

But the next time the train came, the next time the train stopped there, I saw that the boy with the iron charm in his *ghunshi* standing at the edge of the fence. There was another boy with him, slightly older than he was; a zinc *tabeez* on a red thread across his neck. I had once gone to the Bhoorkunda *haat* – heaps of these lay piled on the ground, ready to be sold – piles of sindur, tabeezes, copper, brass, zinc-coloured threads and garlands of beads hanging from bamboo poles. I had seen a salesman plastered all over with dust walking somewhere in the distance towards the Mahato village with innumerable garlands of beads on his shoulders.

The two boys were standing there just beyond the fence, staring awe-struck at the American soldiers. There was an inkling of fear in the eyes of the kid who had come there the first day. His knee was slightly bent in anticipation; he would be off like a deer as soon as he encountered a glance of displeasure.

I was walking around with the form in my hands. Every now and then, I was using whatever excuse came my way, and buttering the Major up. "Awful", said a soldier to the GI next to him as he stood outside the door of his car, sipping his coffee, and saw the two boys.

I had never felt that way. They seem to be happy enough with themselves – they work in the open fields, hunt *khataash* with the catapult or the bow and arrow, listen to *natua* songs, get drunk on *hariya*, and sometimes stop suddenly in their tracks and draw themselves up to their full height, firm and straight as the string of a bow. Thin bodies draped in loincloths, dark, rough. But that GI guy's "awful" seemed to prick me. I felt very angry with the boys.

One of the soldiers launched into a full-throated rendering of a couple of lines of a song. A few of them were laughing boisterously. One soldier drained his mug in a trice and winked at the server-coolie to have it filled again. The guard came forward to see how much longer it would take. The guard was a Punjabi, but he managed to affect a nice nasal note as he talked to the Major.

Then the whistle sounded, the flag was waved, and everyone scrambled onto the train. Even the military police with the wide red ribbon on their arms.

Again that void. The train left; only the barbed-wire fence kept vigil like the *phanimansa* in the sandy emptiness.

Only a few days later, another train arrived. A POW car this time–Italian prisoners of war were being smuggled elsewhere again from Ramgarh. Where to, we didn't know, we didn't ask.

They had their own special striped clothes. Their faces were uncreased by smiles. Their train was monitored at all times and from all sides by men carrying rifles poised to swing into action. Even we used to feel somewhat scared. I had heard in Bhoorkunda that someone had apparently tried to escape, putting on a *dhuti* and a *punjabi* to avoid detection. He had failed. The fact that I was a Bengali gave me an additional reason to be scared.

After the train left, I noticed that it wasn't just the two little boys, a girl of about 15 dressed in a short piece of cloth and two men, had left their work in the fields as well and were standing near the fence. After the train left, they whispered something among themselves, laughed and, gurgling like the mountain spring, went back towards the Mahato village.

One, two, five-the next day, I saw 10 or 12 people from the Mahato village start running as soon as they saw the train. They left their fields behind and came running towards us. I suppose the flicker of khaki at the train window was a tell-tale signal for them. Two passengers would whoosh past like mail trains everyday, a couple of goods trains, too, would rumble past. How come nobody from the Mahato village ever came jostling then, nobody expected the train to stop?

One day I had gone and broached to *Mahatoburo*, the old man of the Mahato village, the idea of having someone sent to our camp at Andahalt to sell vegetables, *chingri, sarputi and maurala*. The old man had smiled and said, "Our fields come first." So, it was with surprise that I looked at the rows of dark loincloth-clad men, those girls in the half-sarees. Only the bare-chested old Mahato had a pair of *tangi* shoes on his feet, shoes made by the village cobbler. They all came and stood in rows near the barbed-wire fence.

By now, the train had arrived. The American soldiers had got down with a flurry and walked in single file, armed with mug and *thali*.

Two hundred and eighteen breakfasts lay ready at BF Three Thirty-two. BF Three Thirty-two, meaning Andahalt.

Winter had just started to make its appearance. The distant mountain had a muffler of mist wrapped round it. The trees and shrubs were a dew-bathed green.

A soldier expressed his delight in his Yankee accent.

Another was standing in front of the car and staring unblinkingly at the barrenness beyond the barbed wire fence. Suddenly, keeping the coffee mug on the steps leading into the train he put his hand into his hip pocket. Taking out a shiny quarter from his bag, he tossed it at the Mahatos. Puzzled, they looked at the soldier, looked at the shiny quarter lying on the *moorum* inside the fence, exchanged puzzled glances among themselves, and just kept on staring in bewilderment.

"Saaheb has given you *baksheesh*. Pick up your *baksheesh,*" I said, seeing that they were going back again quietly after the train had left.

They all looked at each other searchingly; nobody came forward.

I picked the quarter up and handed it over to *Mahatoburo*. He stood staring at me like an idiot; then they all walked off in silence. Not a single word did any of them utter.

I didn't like having to pander to our man one bit. Besides, not a single soul in sight, not a single passenger train stops here, just Bhagwatilal and his three coolies in the tent. It's so very lonely. The soil is barren, the afternoon sky is barren, and so is my mind.

Nobody from the Mahato village would come close either. Once in a while, I would to go and buy vegetables and *chuno*, small fish, from them. They wouldn't come to our camp to sell, but they would walk all of three *kroshes* to the Bhoorkunda *haat*.

For the next few days, nothing happened. Everything was quiet, really quiet.

Suddenly, one day, the boy with the iron charm on his *ghunshi* came and asked, "Where is the train?"

I couldn't help smiling. "It'll come, it'll come."

How can you blame the child? Short, unimpressive hills, arid land – one has to cover two *krosh* on foot through jungles of *khair* to see a crowded village bus. A passenger train would whoosh past in the morning without slowing down the slightest bit, the evening Down train wouldn't stop either; still, we would run out from our tents for a momentary glimpse of a few hazy faces behind the windows. Nobody to talk to, not a single new face; it was a stifling, suffocating experience. Thus, just as the news that the special American soldiers' train was coming would unsettle us, it would also bring us relief.

Only a few days later, first came the news, then, the next day, the Military Special. The GIs scurried down and queued up to get their coffee, eggs and, bread.

I suddenly noticed that the entire Mahato village had gathered just beyond the barbed-wire fence. Twenty, thirty ... you are bound to lose count, what with all those children standing knee-high. The girls in the hitched-up half-sarees too, staring stupidly. The sight made me feel somewhat scared. I used to feel very scared when Bhagwatilal or the seven coolies wanted to go to the Mahato village. There was no platform as such, you know, only a part of the land beside the railway lines raised by strewing *moorum* to help people get on and get down from the train. The American soldiers were sipping their coffee and strolling around, a few of them were staring at the dark people of the Mahato village.

Suddenly, one of them advanced towards Bhagwatilal and took his wallet out of his hip pocket. Out came a two-rupee note from his wallet. "You have coins?" he asked. The soldiers never wanted to carry change in coins around with them. Instead of taking the change from the shopkeeper or the hawker or the cabbie, they would say, "That's okay, you can have it." I'd been to Ranchi a few times and I'd seen all this.

Bhagwatilal was changing the note into annas, two-annas and quarters when I suddenly noticed the boy with the iron charm on his *ghunshi* smiling from the midst of the crowd near the barbed-wire fence; he had his hands stretched out and was asking for something.

The American soldier took the annas and two-annas from Bhagwatilal, and soon, he was hurling a fistful of coins at the Mahatos.

I had got the Supply Form okayed by then. The guard had sounded his whistle. The train had started to move. I turned back at the Mahatos.

They were still standing there, watching. Then, all of a sudden, the boy with the iron charm strung across his *ghunsi* and the boy, with the zinc charm on the thread round his neck, pounced through the barbed-wire fence on the coins lying on the *moorum*.

"Don't you dare," cried out the old Mahato, in his *tongee* shoes, at once. He said it so loudly that even I was startled.

But the boys didn't listen to him. The two of them were

busy garnering as many of the coins as they could.

They were smiling the way a tender young stalk of maize smiles when you peel the covering off. The whole crowd of men and women were laughing. The old Mahato, enraged, let out a unending stream of words at them in their language. The crowd of men and women kept laughing. *Mahatoburo* walked back towards his village alone, grumbling to himself in anger. The Mahatos, too, went back, talking and laughing like a gurgling mountain stream.

When they left, Andahalt went back to its solitary, silent emptiness. Sometimes, it would make me very depressed. Mountains in the distance. *Mohua* jungles. You cross the *khair* bushes and you come across the fall, trickling its way down the hills, and the green fields of the Mahato village. It was all so pleasant. And the dark, sunburnt men in loincloth.

The train of American soldiers comes here often; they have their eggs and bread and mugs of coffee and leave. The Mahatos come en masse. They stand in line beyond the barbed-wire fence.

– *"Saab, baksheesh, saab, baksheesh"*, several rustic voices clamour.

About to get the Form okayed by the Major, I am startled by the sound and look back.

It is not just the boys, I see, some full-grown men, too, have their arms stretched out. A robust young woman in the half-saree, as well.

One day, when I had gone to buy vegetables, this girl had asked, smiling, "When will the train come next?"

Sometimes, without rhyme or reason, they would come in groups and stand around, they would wait and wait and finally leave. A few Americans sporting stripes across their shoulders had, by then, taken out fistfuls of annas and two-annas from their hip-pockets and tossed them at the crowd. They didn't wait for the train to leave, they made a mad scramble for the coins. In that mad rush to reach inside the fenced-off area, some received scratches and cuts on their arms and legs, others ended up with their loincloths in tatters.

After the train had left, I looked at them carefully. It looked as if half of the Mahato village must have gathered there. There was a flush of excitement on every face; everybody had got something or the other. But even though I scanned or the crowd very carefully, I could see the old Mahato with the *tongee* shoes. *Mahatoburo* had not come. The other day, the two boys hadn't thrown back the coins in spite of his protestations and scoldings. That was probably why he had got mad and refused to come back. It felt nice to think that the man was, perhaps, standing alone in the field, and working on it.

Our days, for the five of us, I mean, if you include the cook, Bhagwatilal, were passing by uneventfully in our camp at Andahalt. Sometimes, once in a while, a train full of soldiers would come, wait, and then leave. The Mahatos would come and crowd near the barbed-wire fence. They would all stretch out their arms and shout, "*Saab, baksheesh, saab, baksheesh.*"

On some rare occasion, I would spy *Mahatoburo.* Sometimes, he would leave behind his work on the field, and, dusting the grime off his hands, take great strides forward towards us. Enraged, he would scold all of them. Sometimes, unheard and unobeyed, he would just keep looking at the villagers with a mute protest in his eyes.

But nobody ever deigned to even glance at him. The soldiers would dig into their hip pockets and, laughing boisterously, toss fistfuls of coins at them. The Mahatos would fall upon them in an acrimonious heap; they would snatch at the coins and get into a scrap with each other. This would make the soldiers laugh out loud.

Then I noticed, for several days in a row, that the old Mahato, in *tongee* shoes, was not there. I felt a certain pride to think that the old Mahato was angry with them and was refusing to come back. That was because we – Bhagwatilal and I – would sometimes feel very nettled by the way those men acted. Somewhere deep inside, we would feel ashamed. Seeing their dirty, tattered clothes, the soldiers probably took them to be beggars. I used to feel very bad about it.

That day, they were yelling "*Baksheesh, baksheesh*" from the other side of the fence. I was chatting with Janakinath, the guard in the khaki bush-shirt with the IE on his shoulder. An officer who was walking his way in nice, crisp steps near us, on hearing their shouts, spluttered and spat out the words, "Bloody beggars."

Janakinath and I looked at each other. Our faces darkened in humiliation. We couldn't raise our heads and look straight. We just seethed in impotent rage.

"Bloody beggars, bloody beggars".

All our anger got directed at the Mahatos. As soon as the train left, I rushed towards them with Bhagwatilal by my side. They tucked the coins they had picked up into their waists and ran off, laughing. Still, my feeling of shame for them lay submerged behind a sense of pride. That pride took the form of Mahatoburo who stood tall like a mountain in front of my eyes.

But, that day, all the pain in my heart did a disappearing act. I'd got the news when I went to meet our man in Bhoorkunda.

The two server-coolies were then rolling with their feet the drums that used to double as tables, and were banishing them to the other side of the Andahalt barbed-wire fence. Another was pulling the tent down.

Bhagwatilal gave a powerful kick to the drum and uttered "*Khel khatam, khel khatam.*"

Suddenly I heard a commotion. Startled, I turned back and saw the Mahatos running towards us. We stared at them, puzzled. Bhagwatilal laughed, who knows why. By that time, the villagers had formed a crowd near the barbed-wire fence.

Right at that moment, I heard a whistle The rumble of a train reached my ear.

Turning back, I saw that the train was coming towards Andahalt; khaki uniforms could be seen at the windows.

We were disconcerted. We were bewildered. How is it that the Bhoorkunda office has forgotten to send word? Or, is it that the information I had been given was wrong?

The closer the train approached, the stronger the booming sound got. No not a sound, but a song. It soon became evident that the whole train was singing, Soldiers on the train joining in the chorus and singing at the top of their voices.

Like a man disoriented, I looked first at the train, then at the crowded barbed-wire fence. My eyes immediately fell on the old Mahato. *Mahatoburo*, too, was part of the crowd and shouting with his hands outstretched, "*Saab, baksheesh, saab baksheesh.*"

They shouted like madmen, like beggars. They. And that old Mahato.

But the train of American soldiers did not stop at Andahalt that day, as it used to. Like the passenger trains, it ignored Andahalt and whooshed past. The train would never stop here again, we knew.

The train left. But it left everybody in the Mahato village a beggar. All the men who used to work in their fields – they all became beggars.

Originally published in Bangla as '*Bharatvarsha*'

THE BAIT

Narayan Gangopadhyay

Translated By Suman Ghosh

A parcel arrived in the morning. I unwrapped it and saw a pair of shoes.

No it couldn't be an adversary. Nobody has tried a prank on me by sending a pair of tattered old shoes either. These are a wonderful, sunny pair of new tigerskin slippers. My eyes are soothed at their sight, and I feel justly abashed slipping my feet into them. I want to lay them out on the bed intsead.

But who had sent me this pair of shoes? I cannot even remember having placed such an order anywhere. And I know all my friends quite well, and none of them has the breadth of mind or pocket to make a free gift of such a pair. What, then, could the matter be?

I was thinking whether I should be astonished, when a green

card caught my eye. *With best compliments of Rajabahadur NR Chaudhuri, Ramganga estate.*

And then a chronicle of the jungle, of eight months back – a singular account of a hunting game – came to my mind.

The record of my relationship with the Rajabahadur is hazy, the strands in disarray. As far as I remember, one of my erstwhile classmates was employed in his estate. It was in this connection that I had composed a poetic- felicitation for the Rajabahadur on a celebration of his birthday. I had borrowed from Ishwar Gupta's alliterations to compose this panegyric, one or two lines of which went like this:

> You light up the three worlds O lord of light
> Your prowess, your qualities add to your kingly might
> Your deeds on this earth are unpeered as Rama's
> Slayer of the enemy, you are unique

The benefits of my poetic labours came as instant rewards. I had read that Akbar's courtier Abdur Rahim Khan Khanan, after listening to a four-line composition by Hindi poet Gang, had given him an award of four lakh rupees. I saw that the tradition of the Nawabi temperament was even now upheld by the talented, exalted, rebel-subduing king. On someone like me, who was poorer than the poor, fell the imperial eye; he summoned me, then asked me to tea regularly and once, on a small pretext, presented me with an on a small pretext, presented me with an expensive gold watch. Since that time, I have been extremely grateful to his majesty. I have even started believing the very epithets that I had used in the poem merely to sustain my rhyme.

I respect the Rajabahadur. And it is natural to respect one who appreciates talent. My friends call me a sycophant. But I know that's merely heartburn, they envy my good fortune. But I don't care. If you have to tie a boat, it is better to choose a large tree, at least it can provide complete shelter from the impact of the odd squall or gale.

So, when eight months back, Rajabahadur asked me to accompany him on game hunting, I couldn't refuse. I left all my work in Calcutta and set off in full throttle. Besides, apart from the once-in-a-while sight of British soldiers raising their rifles and shooting down vultures, I had no clear idea of hunting at all. So even from that angle, there was a deep and genuine allurement.

There was a small railway track in the jungle, and an even smaller railway station on it, and here the train stopped. As soon as it did, an orderly in a spotless uniform with a golden crest saluted me. "Come, sir," he said.

On the dirt track outside the station I saw a grand car – the official name for which is Rolls Royce, called in short, 'Rose'. Rose indeed. Whether it drove on the ground, or flew in the air I couldn't quite make out. The seats weren't tough leather ones, but cushions of red velvet. I was loathe to lean back, afraid that my cheap hair oil should stain them. And no later had I sat, did I feel that even if the world were crushed beneath the wheels like a clod of mud, I would still be able to sleep comfortable and unconcerned here.

The 'Rose' floated on like a swan. It was being driven on a dirt track, but there were no jolts. I felt like leaning out to check whether it was actually on the ground or whether its wheels were flying two feet above the ground.

On both sides of the road, a picture of a new world appeared. Intermittently behind the green sal trees was the expanse of the tea garden, a quiet green sea of bright, sparkling leaves. Far away, against the backdrop of the sky were the dark contours of the hills.

Slowly the tea gardens came to an end and uninterrupted forests of sal densely appeared on both sides of the road. An orderly told me, "The forest is here, Sir."

Forest indeed! The rays of the sun had moved away from the track and now there were only calm and sombre shadows. The dew of the night had kept the path moist. Under Rose's silent wheels the dried up sal leaves emitted crackling sounds. In the breeze, like droplets of rain, sal flowers dropped on the roadside, wafted towards me as well. From somewhere, came the piercing momentary cry of a peacock. The eye could see through the dense sal forests in a few places on both sides, while in other places the vision was obstructed by thick bushy growths. Once in a while, there were pieces of wood with

1935, 1940 written on them. Man does not merely want to clear away forests; he wants to expand them as well. In these plots, new saplings had been planted at different points of time, and these were the indicators.

I went along, viewing the beauty of the forest. It wasn't as if I didn't feel afraid, now and then. If the car engine gave in, inside this dense forest, and if a wild animal seized his chance and leapt, then?

I had no other weapon to defend myself but the fountain pen in my pocket.

At last, I could not bear it any longer and asked, "Hey, are there tigers here?" They smiled their commiseration.

"Yes sir."

"Bears?"

That was regal propriety, so they answered only as much as the question demanded, they said, "Yes sir."

"Pythons?"

"You're right, my lord."

At that point, my enthusiasm for questions came to an end. The quick speed with which they answered my questions, it was unlikely that they would assure me by saying no in reply to a question. As far as I understood, gorillas, hippos, vampires – none were absent there. Whether Zulus and Filipinos were aiming their poisoned boomerangs and whether they loved they taste of fried human meat was also a perplexing question which had come to my mind by then. But I restrained myself.

A little further, and the car brakes screeched. I almost yelled in fright, "What's it? A tiger or what?"

The orderlies grinned. "No sir, we've arrived." I looked more keenly. True enough. Without doubt, we had reached. To the left of the road, inside the sal forest, there was a cleared space. On it stood a two-storied bungalow-type timber house, as sudden and as unexpected in this dense forest.

Hearing the sound of the car, two or three attendants hurried out. I hadn't noticed that a moat had been dug in front of the house until now. The men carried a large plank and placed it like a bridge over the moat. The car went on top of it, right in front of Rajabahadur N.R. Chowdhuri's hunting lodge.

Oh! Oh what luck! Rajabahadur himself was standing on the verandah waiting for me. He smiled broadly and said, "Come in, come in, I haven't had tea as yet for your sake."

My head was bent in respect and humility. Words failed me, but I foolishly smiled the grin of gratitude.

Rajabahadur said, "That you would come taking so much of trouble, I couldn't expect. I'm very happy, extremely happy. Come on, come on, come on upstairs."

Could one be a king without such talent? *This* was regal humility.

Rajabahadur said, "Have a bath first and feel refreshed, tea is being made ready. Boy, take sahib to the bathroom."

The forty year old bearded 'boy' was undoubtedly Bengali. But the order was delivered in Hindi, because that was the royal style. The 'boy' took me to the bathroom.

Amazing, but even inside a forest, the arrangements were so perfect! I had never had a bath in such a bathroom before. On the bracket were three or four, freshly unfolded new towels, in three expensive soap cases were three varieties of soap, expensive oils on the rack, lime juice as well. There was a huge bathtub, with a shower from above. A pump fitted to the tubewell down below supplied water for the shower bath here. The arrangements were royal, who could say that this wasn't Calcutta's Grand Hotel?

I finished my bath. On the bracket were well laundered Pharashdanga dhutis, silk lungis, cotton pyjamas. The last seemed least expensive, so I wore it.

The 'boy' was standing outside, he took me to the dressing room. There were mirrors all around the room and it was as if none of the toilette in the world had been left out.

When I emerged from the dressing room, I was called to the Rajabahadur's lounge. Rajabahadur was reclining with his back to a chair, smoking a Manila cigar. He said, "Come, tea is ready."

I had better not describe the 'tea'. There were tea, coffee, cocoa, ovalteen, bread, butter, paneer, fat-enriched cold meat; from plantains to peaches, fruits alone numbered nearly ten.

I ate away whatever I could from that heap. Rajabahadur had a slice of bread, or a fruit. Meaning, he had practically nothing, apart from three successive cups of tea. Then he lit another cigar and said, "Take a look out of the window."

I looked. I had never seen such unparalleled natural beauty in my life. Just below the window, a three – four hundred feet sheer cliff went down, and the house seemed to be hanging in that devilish emptiness. Down below, I could see the thick forest and running through it, the thin blue refulgent line of a mountain stream. As far as one could see, the expansive forest stretched for several acres. On its borders, blue mountains stood guard.

"Marvellous!" The word just came out of my mouth.

Rajabahadur said, "Right. You poets would naturally like this. I, myself, am sometimes tempted to write poetry. But the forest that you see down below is not the safest of places. It is one of the fiercest wildest in the Terai. A kingdom of prehistoric ferocity."

I looked at the forest in fear. One of the wildest! But I couldn't see anything to be afraid of. Four hundred feet below, the huge stretch of jungle looked like a continuous growth of bushes, and the river looked like as strip of brilliant foil. Wondrous green, wondrous beautiful. Unending nature shone in the unending sunlight; the mountain, was as if, drawn in a dark blue. It felt as if the silent, deep forest would draw me to its breast in an embrace on a soft bed of countless leaves if I jumped from above. But –

I said, "Do you hunt *there*?"

"Are you mad? How should I get down? You can see there is a four hundred feet high hill behind. Till date, no hunter's rifle has reached there. But yes, even though I don't quite hunt, but I sometimes go angling there."

Angling? I was open-mouthed. "How do you fish? From that river?"

"That will be revealed later on. If necessary, you will see." Rajabahadur closed his lips in a mysterious smile. "Let us arrange for game hunting now, if we don't get anything we'll try fish. But I don't like it without good baits, and that calls for a lot of trouble."

"I don't understand."

Rajabahadur did not reply, he merely smiled. Then he exhaled some of the aromatic smoke of his Manila cigar and asked, "Do you know how to shoot with a rifle?"

I understood he was trying to hush up the matter. Immediately I controlled my tongue, because asking any more questions after this would not be justified, nor would it be civil. It is against court manners.

Rajabahadur asked me again, "Can you shoot with a rifle?"

I said, "I did air gun shooting in my childhood."

Rajabahadur laughed aloud. "That's right. You are poets, weapons of offense and defense don't become you. I, of course, picked up a rifle at the age of twelve. Why don't you try, its not such a difficult thing."

Rajabahadur rose and went to one side of the room. I followed him and saw that it wasn't just a lounge, but a proper natural museum and armoury. I hadn't seen this because I had concentrated on the dining table thus far, or else I should have noticed it earlier.

All around, there were firearms of various makes. Four rifles, small, big, differently shaped. Two holstered revolvers hung from a hook. Beside it hung an unsheathed long Sheffield sword – its spotless blade shone like the sun. On a thick leather belt were shining brass cartridges for revolvers and rifles. There were three Nepalese knives in embroidered sheaths as well. And on the walls deer-heads, bear- heads, skins of different kinds – tiger, snake, deer. On a table there was a huge elephant head, with two big tusks pointed front. I understood that these were trophies of Rajabahadur's bravery.

Picking up a small rifle from the table, Rajabahadur said, "This is light, but it's a good repeater; you can shoot big game at ease."

To me, of course, they were all the same – light repeaters and Howitzer guns were all the same. But for the sake of preserving gentility, I said, "Great! Then it's an excellent piece".

Rajabahadur held the rifle towards me. "Then try. It's loaded, shoot through that window."

I stepped three paces back in fright. I've made great many bloomers in my life, but I wasn't prepared to increase their recurrence any more. I had heard from a friend, back from the war, his first experience of rifle shooting – he had broken his leg from a fall, and supposedly spent a full month in bed. As far as I knew myself, it was unlikely that my risk would go away with merely a broken leg.

I said, "Let it be for now, we'll try later".

Rajabahadur smiled in subtle derision. He said, "You're afraid now, but once you learn how to hold it, you won't feel like leaving it. When it's in your hand you'll understand how powerful you are. You can easily face all the rascals of…of…" Suddenly his eyes shone brightly. The light smile disappeared and the muscles of the face tightened. "And a rival".

The blood running in my heart turned cold in an instant. Rajabahadur's eyes were wild with malice, he was holding the rifle with a grip so strong as if he intended to shoot someone in front of him. In his excitement, if he made me his bull's eye then –

I stood with my back against the wall in terror. But by that time, the clouds had cleared – royal tempers! Rajabahadur smiled.

"Well, you will be given training later on. Everything is here, so you can have whichever one you fancy. Come, lets sit in the balcony now, lets have some energy."

I'd swallowed the Vindhya mountains for my breakfast, so

what energies he meant to store was difficult for me to understand. But after finishing what he said, Rajabahadur stepped towards the outer balcony. I had to follow.

In the outer balcony there were cane chairs and cane tables. After coming in here, I had sat in so many different types of seats that I had become quite nervous. But sitting on the cane chair I savored a little easy bonhomie. At least *this* was familiar.

And the moment I sat down I understood the significance of the word 'energy'. The attendent was ready and bringing a bubbling glass on a tray, placed it in front of me – the pungent smell of alcohol pervaded the breeze.

Rajabahadur smiled and asked, "Would you like some?"

I replied in humility, "No".

"Then will he get you some beer? It's a drink for women, you won't get drunk."

"No, let it be. I've never had the habit."

"Hmm, you must have won a prize for good conduct." There was disdain in his tone. "I had my first drink when I was fourteen."

The ways of the royalty – everything was supernatural! They were little vipers from the moment they were born. So comment was unnecessary. The tray came and went again, and again. Rajabahadur's sharp bright eyes slowly clouded, shades of pink touched his fair cheeks. Suddenly he looked at me with sodden eyes.

"Okay can you tell me why you aren't a king?"

When you're asked a question like this, there's nothing else to do but bare your teeth, foolishly. So I did that.

"So you couldn't say why?"

"No."

"Can you kill a human being?"

What sort of talk was this? I felt terrorised.

"No."

"Then you can't tell me. You are absolutely hopeless."

He rose and stepped towards his room. And said, "I pity you." I didn't add to the words and sat down there in silence. A little while later I heard sounds of snoring from inside the room. I looked that way and saw he was fast asleep on the chair in his lounge, his mouth open, and a few flies buzzing at his lips.

That very night I had my first hunting experience.

We were sitting inside the car in the jungle. Two dazzling beams from the car headlight had fallen on the narrow path in front and on the sal forests on both sides. Outside the border of this orb, was the impenetrable darkness of a haunted-house in the jungle, primeval malice had risen to its senses all around. In the darkness of the night, I could feel it in all my nerves. Here a herd of elephants were trudging along, demolishing the stones of the hills far away, the python waiting inside the bushes for the unalert kill, droves of deer with their ears cocked for any imminent danger, and inside one of the chasms glittered the eyes of a hungry tiger. In the darkness of the night, the primary life of the forest lay awake.

I sat silently inside the car in hair-raising, fearful anticipation. But the kingdom of violence, the sal forest was immersed in a surprising stillness. Apart from the incessant buzzing of the mosquitoes around my ears, there was no sound. Once in a while a little breeze blew, and a few sal leaves rustled softly. Sometimes came the cries of wild hens, or the sound of a peacock ruffling its feathers in its sleep. It seemed as if the fearful animals of this deep, fearful forest had held their breaths in the hope of a moment when there would be no fear.

We were also waiting. We sat in the car without a sound, there was no way we could speak even a word. The gleaming nose of his rifle placed right beside the engine, Rajabahadur looked before himself like a tiger on the hunt. His eyes were strained sharp, focused on the illuminated straight line of the headlights; the moment an animal dared cross that line the rifle would sound its boom

But the same stillness prevailed in the jungle. It was as if the jungle had gone to rest today, as if the animals had become tired, and had gone off to sleep in the chasms, or taken the shelter of disease. Sluggish time passed on. The radium dial of Rajabahadur's watch shone like a green eye, it was past one thirty in the morning. The alert Rajabahadur was growing steadily restless.

"No, it's hopeless. We won't get them anymore tonight."

From far away came a piercing, yet sombre cry. An elephant's call. The peacock's feather ruffling sounded every now and again. For a moment, an owl screeched, a pack of jackals called to say that night was in, but where were tigers, or the bears? In the dark forest, there were rapid sounds of scampering deer-hoofs – a herd of deer was running away.

But there were no shadows inside the orb of light. The mosquito bites were getting intolerable.

"It's been a futile night." Rajabahadur's voice betrayed all the irritation of the world. "Devil's luck." From the side of his seat he drew a flask and poured the contents with gurgling sounds down his throat, and the pungent, hot smell of whisky spread out slowly.

"Thank heavens," Rajabahadur moved and straightened suddenly. His hand moved like lightning on to the trigger. The kill had arrived.

Even I saw it. Far away, in the orb of light, an animal stood still. With such a bright light falling on his eyes, it had lost its direction and was looking straight at us. Its eyes shone like two lamps.

The driver said, "Hyena."

"Damn," said Rajabahadur, taking his hand away from his rifle, but the next moment he said in a voice of suppressed excitement. "Leave it, I'll kill that rat today."

Boom, the rifle sounded. My ears were deafened, and my nostrils became senseless with the acrid smell of gunpowder. Rajabahadur's aim was unfailing, the animal had been struck down.

The driver said, "Shall I bring it, Sir?"

Rajabahadur made a face and said, "What's the use? Turn back the car."

The green light of the radium dial showed three in the morning.

The car returned to the hunting lodge. Lighting a Manila cigar, Rajabahadur said, "Damn!"

But, surprise – the forest seemed to have started playing antics with us. In the daytime, after a lot of toil, all we had were two wild hens, not even a deer. The same situation prevailed during the night shoot. On three consecutive nights, we tried stopping our car at different places in the forest, but the net result was the bite of innumerable mosquitoes. We did not meet the ferocious animals of the jungle, but got to recognise the mosquitoes. I had no idea till now that such dangerous mosquitoes could exist in any part of the world.

But the mosquito bites were made up by the sumptuous food we had. To tell the truth, despite the failures of the hunt, there was no complain in my mind. Such lavish arrangement inside the jungle was beyond my dreams. I had never tasted such expensive food in my life, never had a bath in a bathroom as marvelous as this, and on the first day, I couldn't even sleep well because the thick velvet bed made me uncomfortable. In the retreat of the deep forest, I was spending my days in the comfort of Grand Hotel – even if the hunt wasn't a success there wasn't even a little harm done. Everyday, I watched the jungle four hundred feet below me as I sipped tea in the lounge. In the morning light, the bright greenery stretched till the horizon in splendid bliss. One of the wildest forests? I couldn't believe it. I watched the shapeless covering of leaves sway in the breeze, a group of birds circling; from here the birds looked like the bees. Just below the window, like a blade of steel, the bluish tint of the river's course, a few pebbles glittered like precious stones. It felt good.

And then my dream broke. I saw Rajabahadur with a Manila cigar burning from the corner of his mouth, pacing inside the room in impatient and restive steps. There was a silent aggression in his eyes and mouth, his cruel lips were taut. Sometimes he would pick up a rifle and then put it down again in disgust, sometimes he would pick up a bhojali and test its edge by pressing the blade on his own hand. Sometimes he would come right to the window and, for some time, look straight down at the jungle underneath. He had not been able to hunt anything of note for three days, his teeth chattered in rage.

Then, he went off in search of energy. He went out to the balcony and loudly ordered: "Peg!"

But having royal dinners at someone else's expense and living in royal comfort wasn't possible for me for many more days. The benevolence of Rajabahadur was of course important, but I had a home and a family in Calcutta, and duties towards them. So I had to speak up on the fourth day.

I said, "Now give me leave."

Rajabahadur had just sipped at his fourth peg. He looked at me with drunken and bloodshot eyes. He said, "You want to leave?"

"Yes, there is work to do…"

"But I haven't been able to show you how I hunt."

"That we can have next time."

"Hmm," Rajabahadur made a muffled sound within his pursed lips. "So you think those rifles, all those trophies of my hunts on the walls, they are all a farce."

I said with fear, "No, no, why should I think that? Hunting has also got to do with fate."

"Hmm, even fate can be changed." Rajabahadur arose. "Come with me."

We both came out. Rajabahadur brought me to the back of the hunting bungalow. Right at that spot, from where one of the fiercest sections of the Terai lay four hundred feet below.

I saw something new here. I saw that a wooden cantilever provided with wooden railings hung out from here into the open space in front, for about 15 to 16 hand lengths. On its sides there were two wooden wheels, with two pairs of thick jute twine rolled around them with hooks attached. I couldn't understand what it was.

"Come," Rajabahadur walked on to the cantilever bridge. I followed him. It was an amazing arrangement. Just at the end of the cantilever was the course of the mountain stream, its narrow pebbled sand banks on both sides, and apart from this, jungle after jungle. Looking down made my head swim. Rajabahadur said, "Do you know what this is?"

"No."

"This is my angling arrangement. This has to be worked secretly, there are many hazards. But it's surefire."

"I can't quite understand."

"You'll know tonight itself. I've asked you for the hunt, I'll show you a new way to hunt. But you can't reveal this to anyone ever."

Without understanding anything, I said, "Okay."

"Then stay till tonight. Tomorrow morning I shall arrange for your car." Rajabahadur began walking towards the front side of the hunting lodge. "After tomorrow morning, as it is, you cannot stay here anymore."

One wooden cantilever, and two things which looked like pulleys. An arrangement for angling. Couldn't tell anybody, and had to leave tomorrow morning. All together, it seemed like the very living room of mystery. I felt everything was in disarray. But I couldn't ask more questions; I was uncomfortable asking the Rajabahadur too many. As if it was out of bounds.

Three or four dirty little children were playing in front of the bungalow. They were the unclaimed property of the Hindustani keeper. Rajabahadur had sent the keeper to the town in the morning, he would be back on the morrow with a few essential supplies. A very faithful and devoted man. Motherless, the children play in front of the bungalow throughout the day. Rajabahadur looked quite benevolently towards them. From the second storey window he threw at them paisa coins, pieces of bread or biscuits. And down below they lunged for them in the air like dogs. Rajabahadur looked at them in amusement.

Even today, the children came and crowded round him and said "Salute, master." Rajabahadur brought out a few coins from his pockets and scattered these among them.

They scrambled for them like manna.

Nice kids. Two to eight years old. I quite liked them. Like the sal saplings of the forest world, they too are lively and fresh, drawing their life force out of the recesses of nature.

In the evening, sitting at the dinner table, I said, "You said you would go fishing tonight."

Rajabahadur looked at me from the corner of his eye. I've noticed throughout today, that he had been drinking too much, and continuously puffing away at his cigar. He hadn't even spoken to me very much. There's something going on inside him.

Rajabahadur said briefly, "Hmm."

"When will it be?" I asked with reticence.

Exhaling a mouthful of smoke from the manila cigar, he replied, "I'll call you when it is time. Now you go to bed. You can sleep peacefully for a few hours."

The last words sounded clearly like an order. I understood that he would rather not converse with me now for very long. The order to get to bed quickly wasn't just a request from the guest-entertaining man of the house, it was an order from the king. It were better I did not delay obeying.

But even lying on that extremely soft rug on the bed did not bring me sleep. Disjointed thoughts did the rounds in my head. Angling, the cantilever, pulleys, all so very secret. Unfathomably mysterious.

Then , as I turned this way and that, I did not even realise, when sleep came to me.

The strong glow of a torchlight woke me up with a start.I did not know what time of the night it was. The forest surroundings were wrapt in solitude. Only the shrill cry of the cricket sounded outside.

There was somebody's ice cold hand on my body. Rajabahadur said, "It is time, come."

The torch sent shivers from my head to foot.

I was about to say something. Rajabahadur put his finger on my lips and said, "Don't talk, come."

This silent beckoning in the deep of night – as if it was the setting for a hair raising novel. Some sort of disturbance, an unknown fear, rattled inside my being. As if enchanted, I came out behind the Rajabahadur.

The hunting bungalow was dark as if wrapped in the coldness of death. Continuous cries of crickets came from all sides of the forest – the rustle of leaves sounded like the wail of the forest. In the late hours of that previous night, I had felt quite afraid when the car stood in the middle of the forest. Tonight, I felt afraid too. But this fear was of a different kind, there was something else which I could not quite understand, my legs wouldn't move. There was a torch beam on my face, the touch of the Rajabahadur's hand felt ice cold, his finger on my lips signalled the unexplained cipher of silence.

Rajabahadur flashed his light and led me towards that hanging cantilever. I saw arrangements for a hunt made on it. Two bearers were lowering something by rotating the wheel of a pulley. For a moment, Rajabahadur flashed his nice cell hunting torch downwards. Nearly two hundred and fifty feet below, a white bundle of sorts was being hurled down at a great speed from the rope attached to the pulley.

I asked, "What is that Rajabahadur?"

"Bait for fish."

"But even now I can't understand anything."

"You'll understand later. Now keep quiet."

This was a clear rebuke. A strong smell of whisky emanated from his mouth. Rajabahadur wasn't in his senses. And still I understood nothing – everything in my head was in a whirl. I sat on the chair beside Rajabahadur like some silent spectator of an incomprehensible play.

On the other side, at the end of the deep dark forest, arose the crescent moon. Some of its pale light shone on the water of the river four hundred feet below, and scattered on the pebbles like semi-precious stones. Hazily I could see, the white bundle tied to the rope moving slightly on the sand. Rajabahadur aimed the rifle with one hand, and with the other shone the light on the bundle. The flash of light indicated that the bundle was, as if alive, but what it was I did not understand. This was supposed to be bait for fish. But what fish – and what was the bait?

Again the silent wait. Seconds passed, then minutes, hours. Rajabahadur's torchlight beamed down below every now and then. The fierce forest stretching to the horizon in half moonlight, seemed a billowy sea. The river below shone bright, like an unsheathed sword. I sat in speechless wonder. Minutes passed, then hours. Rajabahadur sat fishing with his bait.

But everything was cloudy to me. I listened carefully, to the sound of the crickets, the trumpet of the elephants, the rustling of sal leaves. Only the smell of whisky and Manila cigars entered my nostrils. Minutes passed, hours passed, the radium dial of the watch showed its hands rotating. Slowly I fell into a daze, I fell almost asleep. Then suddenly, a rifle cracked with an unearthly sound beside my ear, from 400 feet below shot forth the booming roar of a tiger. I trembled in my chair.

The torchlight shone straight on the pebbled sand bank. I saw the striped, huge animal lying with one of its paws on the white bundle, lashing its tail in final regret, clearly. From above, like Indra's thunderbolt, an unerring bullet had hit its head. That such an unavoidable death would strike him from above, he could not have imagined. Rajabahadur said triumphantly, "It's over."

Now I understood what he had meant by angling. Gleefully I said, " You've caught your fish. Now how will you bring him up?"

"With that pulley. That's why I have arranged for it."

The whole affair was as novel as it was relishing. As I was about to congratulate Rajabahadur. – then, just then – I clearly heard the cry of a little boy. Faint but unmistakable. What was that sound?

The sound had come from four hundred feet below. Yes, there was no mistake. The twine that muffled his voice had come off, just a bit too late. My blood turned cold, my hair stood on end. I cried out like a madman, "Rajabahadur, what have you used for a bait? With what have you caught your fish?"

"Quiet." He pressed the black rifle muzzle on my chest. The next instant, the world around me began to whirl, turned into an air bubble and vanished. If Rajabahadur had not caught me then, I would have gone down those four hundred feet.

If one of the keeper's illegitimate boys had been lost in the jungle, there was nothing unnatural about it. But Rajabahadur had shot a huge Royal Bengal Tiger, one which he could show off to people.

Eight months after that, I've received this pair of slippers. That night, eight months ago, was now at best a bad dream. But these slippers are quite real. I slipped my feet into them and walked a little. So soft, yet so comfortable!

Originally published in Bangla as *Toep*.

JATAYU

Dipendranath Bandyopadhyay

Translated By Debalina Sen

The sound of the train grew fainter and fainter until it merged with the drone of the crickets. Then there was darkness again. Some trees of various forms, smutted together with the sky-earth and emptiness, were scattered here and there in an incredible manner. Even the fireflies weren't there today. It seems on a new moon night like this even the firefly does not glow. The darkness thickened like muck. Deep here, pale there, admitting no play of light and shade. It's the month of *Poush*. Dew condensed like drops of darkness.

And amidst this unbelievable environment, the small gathering looked even more unreal in the light of a few petromax lamps. There was just a canvas shade over the head of the idol. This year too Dasarathi has sculpted the idol. A deep blue body taking shape. Bright red tongue. Large eyes.

From the neck, the hand, hang a few human heads, as if freshly beheaded.

The preparations for the *sandhi puja* have been made. The old priest sat on his haunches on the *kush* mat, entranced, looking at the idol, murmuring incantations, as if chanting a story. At times he heaves a sigh and utters in a broken voice – *Ma, Ma.* The cry, like the wings of the bat, flitted in the dark and disappeared. Four drummers have come. The small boy plays the *kansi*. They sit back, smoking cannabis. A little later they will have to accompany Netyacharan as he dances. Then the sacrifice, and the puja. Their place is right in front of the idol. Eight to ten arm-lengths of ground has been dug, watered and made slippery. It is difficult to walk or even move on it. Netyacharan will fly like a bird over this. There will be brass-pots over his head and between his teeth. In the pot there will be fire. And Netyacharan will twist his body, balance himself on his feet, and dance in a startling manner. He will dance inside the fire. He will dance carrying fire. Netyacharan will become fire.

Over-enthusiastic youngsters are running around, arranging for every small thing. The last minute bustle, the stray shouts seem meaningless in the midst of that strange environment and preparations. Someone, for no reason, dumps more jackfruit leaves in front of the sacrificial goat. The people move backwards even before the flame is lit as if touched by its warmth. The women sit separately. The puja was next to the cremation ground. So there isn't any clamour of young children. Only the village dogs have come all right. They are sniffing the earth and roaming around here and there.

Durga drew the saree over her head. She sat huddled in the last of the rows of women, in a remote corner. Darkness has cast a different shadow on this side. Earlier, on such nights her place used to be right in front, where the mild heat of the fire could be felt, just about. Every posture, every action, every expression of Netyacharan could clearly be seen. Durga looks at the muddy slippery ground unmindfully and tries to think – long ago, I, what was it, I – as if – then she realizes suddenly she cannot really think of anything now. She notices disinterestedly that there is a special regard for her today in the other women's eyes. As Netya's wife, they are treating her with respect. She is surprised; the days of being honoured in Netyacharan's name are not yet over. Immediately her thighs begin to burn. Durga holds her breath, and sits helplessly eyes closed. The fear, that same fear, again, now. Her heart pounded. The tips of her hands and feet wanted to say something in the drone of the crickets.

While returning from work she had seen the man in the crowd at the railway station. He glanced at her, winked his left eye and smiled. Durga turned her face, walking as fast as she could, and boarded a women's compartment. And then all the way she trembled like dry bamboo-leaves. Who is the man? Why did he look at me like that? Why did he smile? Did he wear spectacles? No, he had a thin moustache. Did he wear dhoti or trousers? Couldn't remember, couldn't recognise. I can't recognise. Why did he smile? Does he know me? Which railway station will he go to? Or is he just following me?

At every station, with eyes keen but feigning disinterest, she searched for the man. Then as she got down from the train she suddenly noticed a young man leaning against the railing, striking a match, with which he forgot to light his bidi as he looked at her. Without looking anywhere, Durga started off on her way straight through the field. Was he the same man? But he had no moustache, and he wore pyjamas. Why then did he glance at me? Was he the same man or someone else?

She tried to recollect the faces one by one. But none emerged distinct. She could not remember anybody in particular. An indistinct form floated in a haze in front of her eyes. Durga struggled to identify it. A hairy hand, just a hand, pinched her coarsely on her bosom. Then it throttled her.

The ridge-paths of the field were crowded that day. All of them would attend the puja, watch the dance. On her way Durga could hear Netya's name from various lips, unrelated fragments of stories, true and false. Those who knew her, smiled at her. Those who did not, gave her a look of surprise and began talking in a low voice. And Durga filled with suppressed excitement and doubt every moment, chased by an unknown fear, walked like a beast with hunched shoulders and ears cocked. I can't stand a crowd. I can't bear it. It scares me. I feel uneasy if I see people smiling and talking to each other. I feel like running away if anyone stares at me. A stranger arouses suspicion. My hands and feet tremble if someone I know talks to a stranger. I can't bear a crowd – I feel uncomfortable. I have lost all faith. I can constantly sense a conspiracy. I am certain its web will slowly spread here as well. It will spread slowly. I will be trapped in it. Then a hand will come up, point its finger and say, here, this one. The hand will not move over my body, my tummy, it will not bury its nails in my neck. Even then I shall die. I have to go. Where? I don't know. There was peace in the house. I was living in my own house like a thief. A haughty man like him too spent his days like a thief. They felt for us. We were almost wiped out yet somehow we survived. He came out of the house again today. Dragged me out too. I can't tolerate a crowd. Can't tolerate so many eyes. I fear something might happen. May be today itself. And restless, I will watch every moment. But I should not reveal the anxiety. What shall I do then? Then, I, that man, that hand, will dance. I will watch the dance.

He appeared a hero then.

He was in tight underwear. The slippery bare body glittered. A piece of dirty cloth clung on to his waist like oil in water. Netya carefully made himself up today. He rubbed a lot of soap in his hair to make it fluffy, put a vermilion mark on his forehead and wore rounded beads like ripe rosy berries on his arms and around his neck. There were fine shredded leaves too. His heart swayed in pride. His legs and thighs too have a lot of hair, quite masculine. Muscles all over. He swelled up the muscles and veins – it was quite a sight. Netya was dazed. He kept up an indifferent smile on his stubborn face.

Then the fire lit up suddenly. The blazing flames spread at once. A fence of fire. Netya enclosed in it. Netya's hands are not there. The fence will shrink to a small one by the first-second-third time. Netya is dancing with a fire pot over his head and one between his teeth. He is stepping on the slippery ground slowly, with a lot of affection.

And the sticks began to beat against the drum. Its skin had been tightened in the heat of the fire. The drums decorated with the kingfisher's feathers seemed to hold a royal parasol over the head of a non-Aryan dancing figure, carved out of rock, blazing in the flame of the fire. The *kansi* beat with a shrill, intense sound. The old priest shouted in a broken voice, *Ma, Ma*. The sacrificial goat cried out of fear and began chewing the jack-fruit leaves. And the dogs began to howl and scratch the earth.

Durga gazed at the fire. Fire at the heart of the earth. Fire at the heart of darkness. A hundred colours spiralling in the fire. And smoke. The darkness quivered, fire quivered, smoke quivered. The drumbeat too had begun to quiver.

I had not seen so much fire for such a long time. Dancing was there in his family. No one imagined he would dance this time. The whole year is spent in disgrace out of some fear and foolishness- his wife earns his food – today he stood with his chest puffed up like in those days. People watched him in admiration. And I felt ugly. I detested it. I could clearly see the stitches in his elbows in the flame of the fire. Oh, does he have no shame. Must have plotted something. I don't trust him. What more does he want? Oh, what do you want! Why did he come down to dance making a mockery of me in front of everybody! Does he suspect something? Suspect. He will. What! Then I on that day – that day, I, the same day, fire – more fire – the entire house burnt down. They threw Baba into it. He was running from one room to another. His hair, beard, caught fire. Baba went on pulling out his dhoti till it came out. All his life Baba had been from village to village, singing *katha* . But no hero from the *puranas* came like a wind to save him. They did not let Baba come out. And when the sky was pierced with the monstrous scream from Baba's melodious voice, the cracking sound of the bamboos, and the call of *Aajan*, they lay me in the open field in the light of the burning house. My mother beside me. A hand began pinching my bosom. The burning ashes from the house blew into my eyes. I was feeling hot, yet I shivered with cold.

Ma, Ma. The old priest screamed again.

Durga looked at him startled. It has been long since I called someone *Ma.* I faintly remembered him, sitting here. Here beside the cemetery, this side of the river. I lost my mother, my father, my country. *Ma* did not get any fire in her mouth.

It has been long since I called someone *Ma*! What is the old priest screaming? Who will reply? Does anyone respond? Ever? Then why has this happened to me? Why? When I ran away and stayed in the station, Netyacharan and I got married. Then they forcibly cut the jungle and extended the village. Houses came up. The whimsical arrogant man went about with his chest up, daringly. Even on this side of the river he feared nothing, nobody. But I died of terror even while I lived with him. The fear of that hand haunted me! I could see the hand clearly. Cracked rough palm, black nails, veins swelled up like worms, intending to crush my new shelter. Wants to set me like an accused before two innocent trusting eyes. It played with me and pinched my bosom. In sleep, so often I screamed out, scratching Netyacharan's hand. He kept his hand on my head and calmed me down. With all his stubborness he uttered, we shall again have everything, here, on this side. He used to console me like my mother. It has been a long time since I called someone *Ma*.

Ma, *Ma*! The old priest screamed again. And all of a sudden the drumbeat became faint. Someone from outside threw a bundle of jute stalks. With incredible skill, Netya set fire to the second fence. The fire spread at once. The two fences of fire burnt in circles. Netya danced in the middle. The drumbeat gradually became louder, quicker. The *kansi* beat with a clanging sound. And the goat started calling out of fear. The reflection of the fire quivered in the eyes of the goat. And in that darkness, the idol of Kali, the drumbeat, the shadowy men and women, Netyacharan's eerie dance in the middle of the enchanting fire, the monotony of the goat's cry, created a beastly trap all around.

Someone whimpered softly close to my ears. In moments of intense emotion this man had a habit of beating his chest. Someone was sobbing. *Bou*, I cannot go out in the street without hands. Netyacharan could not beat his chest that day. *Bou*, what will you eat? Could not beat his chest. *Bou*, I sit at home and you go out for a job? Could not beat his chest. *Bou*, no one will call you *Ma*? Could not beat his chest. *Bou*, what do you do till so late at night? *Bou*, why have you eaten betel leaves? *Bou*, how do you get new sarees so often? *Bou*, I know none other than you. Someone was sobbing softly.

The sound gradually became clear. It crossed the distant bridge with a deep booming sound. A goods train with only the light in front, fire in the engine, and some men. He bent down and looked this side.

Netyacharan looked at the train with an inexplicable wonder as he danced. His steps grew quicker without him realizing it. Unknowingly the drumbeat grew faster. Unknowingly, everyone joined the old priest and cried out *Ma, Ma*. A stunned Durga watched the pot fall off Netyacharan's head, as if he would shake off all that was needless in utter disgust. The howl of the dogs surpassed the cry of the goat and echoed in the air. The sound of the train was clear, as if Durga would be able to touch it with her outstretched hands. Black stonechips, wooden slippers, shining rail lines. The wheels of the train rolled away. The nuts and bolts jangled. The two rail lines shook violently. The train rushed. There were two-three bundles of betel nuts tied to the stomach, chest and back. There was a signal near the bridge, perhaps the train would be stopped and searched. All the goods were being tied and hung under the running train compartments. The two lines shook violently. The stone chips shook violently. The wheels of the train, nuts and bolts jangled and clattered. And then suddenly, simply all of a sudden, perhaps, Netyacharan slipped. He fell in the gap between the tracks, and so did not die. Either out of fear or obstinacy he wanted to pull the train to a halt with his hands. The iron wheels tore off one of his wrists and a wing. Then again someone moaned softly close to the ears. Why did this happen, *Bou*, why? Someone was crying. I have not committed any sin. Someone cried, *Bou*, *Bou*, oh, *Bou*. The sound of the train fused with the drumbeat like a deep sigh. And again, for some reason, everyone screamed out in a fierce yet anxious voice, *Ma*, *Ma*.

Netyacharan was dancing in the middle of the two feet wide fire. At times the fire and the smoke screened Netyacharan out of view. He stepped on the thick slippery mud. Sweat all over the body. A little while ago he appeared a hero and now the sight of him dried up the heart. Because his eyes were red and there was that arrogant indifferent smile in his face. The bare haughty body, with no hands, looked as if a man from the *puranas* has come down to earth. There was the chariot of fire in front. The idol of Kali bit her tongue in shame.

Someone threw jute-stalks again. Netyacharan set fire to the third fence. Now the flame was inside the mud as well. There were just about a few yards of space for dancing. It seemed as if fire was coming out from his body. Some screamed out, terrified. Some stood up in excitement. The old priest screamed *Ma, Ma*. This time no one joined him. The goat struggled to free itself. Its dry tongue stuck out. And the dogs howled. Dogs too get terrified. They howl.

Someone gripped the neck hard. She looked up with dazed eyes and saw the youngest bride from the fourth son's family. She didn't know he was gripping Durga. Someone uttered near the ears, *rakshushi*. As if waking up from sleep Durga turned around to see there was nobody. Someone said, it is due to your sin. Someone said, I'll die. Durga tried to stretch out her hands and hold the two feet. The pair of hands lay back on her lap softly like two dry leaves.

The drummers too danced in excitement. Sweat poured down the rock like bodies. The old priest began to dance in front of the idol. The man from some other village, who sat in the men's row watching her for a long time, seemed to come that way, slowly, dancing and swaying his waist. Durga suddenly realized that all men and women had begun to dance. And the fire, red, yellow and purple, danced in three circles. The smoke danced. Grey, brown, black. Smoke covered the fire. The smoke bellowed out. Turned dusty. The curtain in the hotel blew up. Turned dusty. Both the entrances to the cabin were blocked from within with a pair of chairs. A fan moved over the head. Even then she felt very hot. Yet she shivered with cold. She could see the house burning in front of her eyes – Baba running from this room to that, unable to come out-the call of *Aajan* – burnt ash fell into the eyes. Then the sound of the train, wheels rolling over the tracks, the clattering of nuts and bolts – with both his hands he wanted to stop the train – burnt ash fell into the eyes. A radio was playing on the hotel counter, and then that hairy rough hand tickled the neck – a ring in the finger. Durga gripped her neck with all her might and tried to scream.

No one heard her. A train with a fierce sound rushed past within a moment casting ghastly shadows of light and darkness over the tracks at the back like *maydanab* being chased away. And fire danced in the three enclosures. Netyacharan danced, all men and women danced. The drumbeat danced.

He seemed to shout from within the enclosure, *Bou*?

What is it?

Come, let's die.

Oh no. I'm afraid of dying.

Then what do we do?

You say.

Shall we live on like this?

Yes, then at least you will be living.

You will live on like this?

I don't know.

Shall we live on like this?

Yes. At least we shall be alive.

Bou, you will live like this?

I can't take it anymore.

Then what do you say?

I can't take it anymore.

Come, let's die.

I can't take it anymore.

Durga kept on murmuring, I can't, I can't, I can't, I can't. Someone whispered in the ears again, *rakshushi*. Someone said, because of your sin. *Ma, Ma*. Cried the old priest. A lot of them joined him with trembling voices out of fear, devotion and excitement. And Netyacharan's eyes were then Kali's tongue. His entire body seemed to break out in sweat. His steps on the mud became uneven. It seemed he would tumble down any moment. He dropped the pot from his mouth. The fire in the last enclosure was close to his body. There was fire in the mud, fire in the heart of earth. The fire blazed. It danced as it blazed. It danced with uneven steps as it blazed. As if he would tumble down any moment. The amputated elbows looked strange. A tired, out-of-the world spirit seemed to somehow flap its wings. And the stray-dogs, along with the sacrificial goat went on crying.

Durga saw the progressing fire meandering like a snake. The three fences of fire became one. The three creations became one. And someone from within the fire arose and announced, here I am. I know. You could not deceive me. Durga knelt down, dazed. Netyacharan was out of sight. Their colony was burning. Then the fire-chariot sped towards Kolkata. The curtain of the cabin in the hotel where she worked burnt down. The fire like a cruel dictator burnt down everything around. A crying child ran away with a doll in its hand. The fire spread. The people frantically ran towards the river. The river had dried up into a desert. The country had turned to a desert. The whole earth had turned to a desert. The fire ran towards her. Where could I go? Ashes flew into my eyes. Durga felt very hot. Yet she shivered with cold. She murmured, who could have given me such a huge burden! I didn't want you to die, never. There was so much that I desired from life!

Durga then clearly saw her destiny stand in the middle of the fire. The face of the enemy, not clear to her, but the fear of which made her tremble every moment – now, in the form of Netyacharan, lifted up his broken wings to Durga and said, "Here, here, over here."

Originally published in Bangla as *Jatayu*.

TWO THUGS

Moti Nandi

Translated By Sayantan Dasgupta

Sumitra aborted in the middle of the night.

She had been suffering from smallpox for the last six days. Her temperature soared to one hundred and three. Nikhil had been sleeping on the floor. Sumitra's screams woke him. There was Sumitra, sitting terrified on the bed and screaming, "I'm losing it, I'm losing it."

Nikhil switched the lights on and saw the bulge under the saree between Sumitra's thighs. The bulge lurched violently as soon as Sumitra made a slight move. Sumitra has been pregnant these last six months. She was staring at Nikhil with a blank expression in her eyes. Nikhil had to look away. Pockmarks had gouged out parts of her face. Ma was sleeping in the next room; he went and shook her awake.

The landlord's wife came downstairs and advised him to get a doctor. Nikhil woke the neighbourhood doctor and brought him home. He cut the cord, took twenty five rupees and went away. Eight more days to payday at the office, Nikhil calculated. And medicine doesn't exactly come free. There's nothing to worry about, the doctor had declared. Which meant no more money would have to be spent. The bedsheet and the mattress were dripping blood. Sumitra's petticoat had turned red; her saree bore large splotches of blood too. They would have to be discarded. Ma has changed Sumitra's clothes and has dumped the sheet, the petticoat and the saree in one corner, and with them, that thing that had come out from Sumitra's womb.

As soon as the sweeper arrived, the landlord's wife told her to dispose of those things. She took one look at the heap and shook her head. It's too risky; the police would put her in jail if they saw her. She couldn't be persuaded even with the lure of a ten-rupee *baksheesh*. Then the landlord's wife went to confer with the landlord and came and told him, "Get a certificate from the doctor. The police won't say anything if you have it. It's not something shed in shame by some unmarried girl or some whore," he'd said. "It's an accident that has overtaken a married woman from a respectable family."

Following her advice, Nikhil rushed to the doctor. The doctor was not home, and there was no telling when he would return. Nikhil returned home, placed his seven-month baby on the bedsheet and made a neat, little bundle of the baby, the sheet, the saree and the petticoat. He tore off the border of the saree and tied up the bundle as tight and as small as possible. Then he rolled newspaper sheets all over the bundle. Now, it looked exactly like a pack of clothes. Only a few days ago, they had bought the cloth for the curtain and some blouse-piece material from Handloom House. The bag with the name of the shop printed on it was still lying around. Nikhil pushed the bundle into the bag and stowed it away under the bed. Sumitra was lying on the bed, looking at him. Now, she cried out, "But the saree can be cleaned and worn again. Only a small part of it has been soiled." Nikhil didn't pay heed. He didn't even look at Sumitra. Smallpox scar tissues covered her face – they look swollen and ripe and ready to burst open. Nikhil went to the doctor's house again at around twelve-thirty. The doctor was having lunch. He sent his son out with the certificate. "Baba has it all written out," the boy smiled and said.

The way he said it, it seemed, as if, he meant, see – such a clever man; he has made it out even before you asked. But I've paid him a twenty five rupee fee – Nikhil had not forgotten. He left without saying thanks. He is not used to waking up so early in the morning – his eyes were hurting. He had lunch and forthwith lay down on the floor next to Sumitra's bed. Ma had gone to the purohit's house to arrange for a Satyanarayan puja. Nikhil drifted off to sleep calculating how his Casual Leave account stood.

Nikhil had a cup of tea in the evening and then went out with the bag. He checked his pocket several times to make sure he had the doctor's certificate.

The moment he stepped from the alley onto the main street, Nikhil paused. What next? Sparkling lights everywhere, so many people, so many cars. What if he were to dump the bag somewhere here? So thinking, he put it down.

A man appeared at once from somewhere. "Through with your Puja shopping already?" he asked. The man worked in a laundry nearby. Picking up the bag, Nikhil shook his head and resumed walking. The pretty bag would attract attention if he left it there. Some of his neighbours may be around too. After some time, maybe somebody would pick it up. As soon as they saw what was inside, they would raise the alarm and inform the police. The man who'd just seen him would then volunteer, "I know the man, I know the man; he lives in 26/2 in our neighbourhood, he's called Nikhil Chatterjee, works in a bank." Then the policeman would pick up the bag and make an appearance at his house, followed by a horde of onlookers, waiting to watch the fun and spread all kinds of rumours. The very thought of it made Nikhil feel suffocated. He walked into the children's park and sat down on a bench with the bag on his lap. He looked around carefully to see if he could spot anybody he knew. He didn't see anybody he knew, but it was quite possible that there was somebody around who knew him.

He called out to the peanut vendor and bought an anna's worth of peanuts from him. Chewing his way through the pack of peanuts, he began to ponder over how he could be rid of the packet without getting into a hassle.

It would be dark soon. If he could just dump the bag in some deserted alley or field, maybe a mile or two away, and that would be the end of his troubles. The thought reassured Nikhil. He called the peanut vendor and bought another anna's worth; he even haggled with the vendor and made him part with a couple of extra peanuts.

It is difficult to sit quietly all alone in one place for too long, particularly if the scene – the children at play, the affected stateliness of the adolescent girl's walk, rows of spent faces seen through the window of buses plying office-goers home, the lonely young lady, bent forward with her elbow resting on the verandah, the rickshawallah's shoulders bathed in sweat – is such a mundane one. Nikhil thought of the man from the laundry. Not a single time have his trousers come back from the laundry with all the buttons intact. The last time, he had to take them to task over the identification mark put on his shirt. The mark was plainly visible. At this point, Nikhil suddenly remembered that in a detective novel, he had read in his childhood, the laundry identification mark on a piece of cloth had led the detective to the murderer. The man at the laundry must have marked Sumitra's saree and the bedsheet as well. Which meant that wherever the packet was dumped, the police would easily be able to trace the thing back.

Now, Nikhil broke out in a cold sweat. Had it been a child, of even one, or thereabouts, then it could have been taken out in full view of everybody to the crematorium and laid out on the pyre and cremated. But you can't do that to an unformed mass of flesh. The other option was to throw it into the Ganga. But, what if somebody saw him doing it? They'd raise a hue and cry and get a big crowd mobilised. So many questions, they would ask. And, after all that, they'd call in the police. No easy task getting them to believe me. Even if I showed them the certificate, why should they believe me? Who could tell whether what I had thrown into the river was that or whether I had murdered somebody, sliced him up into little pieces, tied up the pieces in a packet and thrown them in?

Nikhil began to feel faint. Only if somebody, taken in by the pretty bag, were to steal it. Surely, the thief wouldn't go and inform the police. Nikhil looked this way and that in search of a thief and was quite astonished to find that there was not a single person around who looked as if he could be a thief. And, to think that on a normal day, he would meet at least a dozen or so who looked suspiciously like thieves to him. In fact, while everybody had suspected the maid when the watch was stolen from the house, Nikhil hadn't had to look even that far – the first face that floated up in front of his eyes had been that of the landlord. But now, he couldn't even find a single thief.

Surely, it can't be that there are no thieves in Calcutta. Perhaps, it's just that there none of them here at this moment. Nikhil stood up, bag in hand. If he wandered about with the bag, surely he would attract some snatcher or a robber. But then, such people are to be found only on dark, deserted streets. Nikhil sat down again and waited for it to get properly dark.

When it was well and truly dark, Nikhil began walking aimlessly. He came across several dustbins where the bag could be dumped. But, a certain fear had struck root in his mind, who knows who would see him – perhaps some young man kissing a neighbourhood girl in a dark alley, or an old lady telling her beads in some dark verandah, perhaps a housewife peering out from her kitchen. A yell, that was all it would take. And, even if that did not happen, well, the identifying marks on the clothes were always there. The investigations of the detectives of the police department would lead them to their target. Of course, one could show them the certificate and say, this was no dark, unlawful deed, *moshai*! The landlord may look like a thief, but even he had called it an accident, not some deliberate act. It can happen to anybody. But long before any of this could be said, the presence of the police would have started a series of whispers in the neighbourhood. Rumours would have begun doing their rounds. Only a few months ago, a sergeant had visited the neighbourhood, and immediately the news of the moment was that Debobrotobabu had been arrested because he used to gamble at home. Finally it was revealed that Debobrotobabu owned a rickshaw and he had been called to the police station because his rickshaw had been in an accident.

All the walking made Nikhil tired. Nobody accosted him with unsheathed daggers to snatch the bag. Yet, he had gone into every *bustee* he had come across. Nobody had even turned to look at him. He walked through several nearby deserted streets as well. A woman from the maidservant class threw him an appraising glance – that was all, nothing else happened. "Now, what?" Nikhil was forced to think.

He began to feel really scared now. So, what is he to do with this seven-month-old dead foetus? It's fifteen or sixteen hours gone already. It would soon begin to rot and stink. If only it had spent the entire term inside Sumitra's womb before making an appearance! Of course, it's nobody's fault. Yet, such an innocent thing as this has put him in a fix. Nikhil felt very angry, too. And, he also realized that he was actually a terrible coward. Quite spineless. Surely, this was not the first time something like this has happened in Calcutta. Those who had been through this must have somehow got out of it. But they are different, Nikhil explained to himself. Human beings are essentially different from each other. They must have been brave people, at least braver than I am.

It suddenly dawned on Nikhil that he would be rid of this menace if only he could dump it on someone who was a greater coward than him. Such a coward would not dare approach the police. He would wander about with the bag and mull over ways to get rid of it. Of course, that greater coward must be saddled with the bag secretly; if he knew whose it was, he would carry it back and return it.

Nikhil stopped at a tram stop and went over the list of people he knew – who, among them, would qualify? A number of names cropped up. He began to go over instances of their cowardice. Finally, he decided on Sasanko. Sasanko had been Sumitra's tutor for almost four years. A marriage proposal had been made to him on behalf of Sumitra's family. But Sasanko had come up with various excuses and opted out. He was the one who had introduced Sumitra to Nikhil. Anyway, Sasanko had got married six months or so ago. If he were to make an appearance now before Sasanko, then surely thoughts of Sumitra, memories of their affair and his refusal to marry her – the entire gory story – and his marriage to somebody else, would surely plant a seed of guilt in his mind. Can there be a greater coward on earth than a former lover? If he could somehow unload this bag into Sasanko's hands, it would be his problem – from then on. In fact, it would be an apt sentence for his betrayal of Sumitra.

These thoughts made Nikhil feel lighthearted. Still, his doubts did not leave him entirely. Sasanko's house was on a small street; he lived on the ground floor. A maidservant answered Nikhil's knocks on the door. Sasanko came out wearing a lungi and *genjee*, a sleeveless undershirt. Recognising

Nikhil, he welcomed him loudly and enthusiastically escorted him inside.

"Sandhya, quick, come and see who is here." As soon as Sasanko uttered those words, his wife came out. Average looks. Sings for the radio, has a few records as well. Nikhil stood up and folded his hands in a namaskar.

"I've heard of you from him." This really had Nikhil stumped. Would the cowardly Sasanko have talked to his wife about Sumitra's husband? Or, was this perhaps just a way of initiating conversation?

"I have briefed Sandhya about all my friends, so, there is no need to elucidate all your talents in a formal introduction."

Sasanko settled into a recently purchased cane chair and began to swing his legs rhythmically. The fact that all the furniture had been bought after their marriage was evident from the new-look lustre emanating from them.

"Her talents, too, we are all aware of, even if you don't tell us." Nikhil used 'we' deliberately. Sandhya, too, playing the role of the modest hostess, responded as she was expected to. "Talent, my foot. Singers like me are a dime a dozen etc.," a certain satisfied pleasure in her voice. Amidst all this, Nikhil tried to ascertain Sasanko's state of mind and started working on a plan. "Now that I have visited you, you must also drop by one of these days."

"Definitely." It was as if Sasanko had been waiting for just such a proposal. "When should we go, tell me – next Sunday?

You'll have to feed us *ilish*. My stomach is sick and tired of *talapia* and Sumitra makes some wonderful *ilish-bhaate*."

Nikhil couldn't help laughing. Sandhya feigned alarm and said diplomatically, "This is not the season for *ilish* and there you go demanding it just to harass the gentleman."

"Come on, he's not a gentleman. He is Nikhil. Sanat and I used to pull his leg the most. Sanat has written he will come to Calcutta in January if he can manage the leave. Don't forget to give me your address – I'll send it to him." Sasanko went on talking at length about Sanat, leaving Nikhil confused.

"That's your Puja shopping, is it?" Sandhya asked all of a sudden. Nikhil smiled a shy smile and shook his head. "Let me see what saree you've bought for your wife," Sasanko said as he pounced on the bag. Nikhil quickly grabbed his hand. "Oh, it's nothing. A *thaan* for Ma, a cheap one from the mill for the maidservant and a 16-rupee handloom saree for Sumitra. Please don't open it. It's all wrapped up, why make me do it all over again?" "Sandhya, look what you are you missing. It has his wife's saree, so he won't even let anybody touch the packet. What colour did you choose? Slate or deep maroon? Sumitra once wore a maroon saree with green dots and a white border – she looked really beautiful."

"She's very fair, isn't she?" Sandhya looked curious.

"No, not very. She has your complexion."

"O Ma, then she's quite dark."

"If you are dark, then we must be like tar."

Nikhil looked at Sasanko with a smile that solicited support. Sasanko nodded his head emphatically. "Oh, no! I've forgotten to serve tea," Sandhya said, evidently pleased with the compliments paid to her complexion.

As soon as Sandhya left the room, Nikhil said, "Sasanko, I'm in a tight spot." Sasanko looked at him questioningly. Nikhil told him the whole story from the beginning, pointed to the paper packet on the table and said, "It's in there."

Sasanko sat up ramrod straight." What! How dare you put that disgusting thing on my table! Remove it, remove it, I say," he hissed, gnashing his teeth and pointing to the floor. Nikhil put it down.

"I don't know what to do with it."

"Throw it away. Throw it into a dustbin, what else?"

"Very easy to say so. The moment you try to do it, somebody will see you. Then, there'll be the shouting; a crowd of people will surround you and then they'll drag you all the way past thousands of people to the police station. They'll say all kinds of filthy things."

"So what do you want me to do?"

"Get this thing taken care of, Sasanko, please. I married her on your request. Now, you keep my request." Nikhil reached his hands out to clasp Sasanko's hands. Sasanko withdrew his hands before he could do so. Nikhil's hands lay spurned on the table.

"So you married her on my request? You didn't fancy her?"

"Certainly. I was in love with her; I still am. But I also know that she had a relationship with you."

"So you have come to dump this on me in exchange." Sandhya walked in with the tea as Sasanko pointed at the bag.

"What exchange?" Sandhya asked smilingly as she settled into a chair.

"Nikhil wanted to hear you sing a couple of songs. So I told him he would have to give you his wife's saree in exchange."

"Oh, come on, he has bought it so lovingly for his wife ... and the songs I sing are hardly to anything to talk about."

Sandhya is a nice girl. She didn't have to be coaxed too much after that. She sang three songs, all without the support of any music whatsoever. Then, Sasanko stood up and said, "I'll walk Nikhil part of the way. Bring me the punjabi."

The two of them began to walk silently, side by side. It was quite late. The streets were almost deserted. The shops had closed, there was little light. It suddenly occurred to him that he could dump the bag anywhere on the way and walk off, unchallenged.

"Here, give it to me," Sasanko stopped in his tracks.

"Why?"

"I'll throw it into that dustbin."

"That, I could've done if I'd wanted to. Why would I have come to you?"

"Then what are you after?" There was a sudden change in Sasanko's voice and his posture. Nikhil stepped back gingerly. Only the *paan* shop in the distance was still open. If he were to run now, bag in hand, he was sure to be taken for a thief and caught. Nikhil stood his ground.

"You are now Sumitra's legally married husband." Sasanka grabbed him by his shirt. "You are the legal guardian of this thing and you have the certificate for it in your pocket. Therefore, all responsibility for it rests with you. I have been free of my responsibility for a long time. Why have you then come to me?" Sasanko began to shake Nikhil.

"You have saddled me with the responsibility. You are a coward, you are irresponsible." The deserted road wrapped in darkness made Nikhil desperate. He shoved and tried to free himself from Sasanko's grip. His efforts were met with a tight slap from Sasanko. Mad with rage, Nikhil jumped into battle in earnest now.

Suddenly, the window above flung open, and a male voice roared from the first floor, "How dare you! You thugs! Fighting on the streets, huh?" The man began to shout. The sound of several people running hard towards them reached them through the darkness.

Nikhil did not give himself any more time to reflect. He began to run towards the more deserted part of the road as hard as he could. When his lungs wouldn't allow him to run any more, he stopped. A constable doing his rounds walked up to him and asked him why he was panting so hard. A thug had been after him, Nikhil explained. The constable wanted to know where the thug was. Nikhil pointed with the fingers. The constable followed the direction of his finger with his eyes, stood there for sometime, then said, "*Achha, theek hai,*" and went his way.

Nikhil now noticed that the paper packet was no longer with him. It hadn't been with him when he was running, either, it had remained with Sasanko. If people asked Sasanko, he would probably say a thug had been after him. Surely, the thug would not have left behind the attractive paper bag with a packet of clothes inside. The men would feel very happy and compliment themselves for having arrived in time to prevent the gentleman from going robbed of his precious belongings. After that, they would hand the bag over to Sasanko.

Nikhil slipped his hand into the pocket near his chest and felt the certificate – he felt reassured. And he saw in his mind's eye, Sasanko, marching with the bag in his hand.

Originally published in Bangla as *Gundadyoy*.

Notes

Aamra	A tree which produces a sour, edible fruit of the same name. *Spondias mangifera.*
Aao mere laal	Come, my darling (child). This is in Hindi. Therefore, the phrase has been left untranslated to retain the element of distance between this phrase and the rest of the text in the original.
Abba	'Father' in a form of Bangla more common in eastern 'Bengal', now Bangladesh.
Alur charchari	A relatively easy-to-cook semi-dry potato dish popular in Bengal.
Aparajita	A flower of a creeper-like plant. It is either blue or white in colour.
Assheora	A type of shrub. *Limonia pentaphylla.*
Aswatha	A large tree having religious significance. *Ficers reliogiosa.*
Atap chal	Rice which has been divested of its husk by merely drying and pounding without previously boiling it.
Atta	Wheat flour.
Babla	A small tree/ shrub common throughout India. *Mimosa arabica.*
Baksheesh	Tips.
Basak	A medicinal plant. *Dhatoda vasica.*

Beaii	Can refer to either son's or daughter's father (in 'Dacoit's Mother', it refers to the daughter's father).
Bedana	A large pomegranate.
Behesht	Heaven. The word is of Persian origin.
Bel	Thorny tree and fruit of the same name, believed in Bengal to be a resting place for ghosts. *Aegie marmelos.*
Bhakt	Devotee.
Balai shaat	A statement used with the intention of preventing an evil/ tragic event, that has been enunciated, from happening. It serves as a kind of prayer, or wish.
Bimaari	Disease.
Brahmin giant	A " great Brahmin ghost" would perhaps be a more accurate translation- because " giant" is used in the sense of "big'- and not in the conventional Western sense of, say, "the Selfish Giant."
Bou	Literally, can mean wife or daughter-in-law or bride (in 'Dacoit's Mother', it refers to Saukhi's wife).
Boudi	Elder brother's wife.
Bouma	Daughter-in-law.
Bustee	Slum.
Chacha	Literally, it means father's younger brother.

The word is also used sometimes to address a man older than the speaker even when he is unrelated to him/ her.

Channamrita — This word is a derivative of 'charanamrita', the 'holy water' given to devotees after puja. Charanamrita is a mixture of water and milk that has been used to bathe the deity's feet (literally, 'charan' means feet, and 'amrita' means nectar). It is expected to be drunk by devotees.

Chhagol — Goat.

Chingri — Shrimps

Chikan — Fine, intricate embroidery.

Chital — A large freshwater fish.

Chuno — Tiny fish.

Dada — Elder brother.

Dahuk — A water bird. *Tringa goensis.*

Dahuki — A female dahuk.

Dakini — A 'mother' form of the female ghost. It is reputed for casting spells on men.

Didi — Elder sister.

Durgabaari — Pavilion for the worship of the goddess Durga.

Ekadashi — Eleventh day of each fortnight of a lunar month; a day marked out as holy and designated for fasting by Hindu widows.

Falgun	The eleventh month of the Bengali calendar (from the middle of January to the middle of February).
Fursat	Time, or leisure.
Gamchha	A cheap, water-retentive, thin towel commonly used in rural Bengal.
Gehnnum	Hell. The word is of Arabic origin.
Genjee	Vest worn by men on the upper part of their body.
Ghentu	A type of wild flower from the plant of the same name.
Haat	(Weekly) village market.
Halal	To kill an animal in the manner prescribed to make it lawful food for Muslims. This word is of Arabic origin.
Haritaki	A kind of myrobalan. *Terminalia chebula*.
Hariya	Country liquor.
Himsagar	A type of mango.
Hortoki	See Haritaki.
Humesha	Always. This word is of Persian origin.
Huzoor	Literally, 'the presence'. A title of respect. 'Sir' is a not too satisfactory approximation in English.
Ilish-bhaat	Hilsa and rice; a delicacy in Bengal.
Indra	King of the gods in the Hindu pantheon. He

	wields as his weapon, *Vajra*, the thunderbolt, and sits on *Airavat*, his mount.
Insaaf	Justice. This word is of Arabic origin.
Jaam	A purple-coloured berry. *Eugenia jambolana.*
Jaishtho	The second month (May-June) of the Bengali calendar. It comes after *Baisakh*, and is followed by *Aashar*.
Jamrul	A white-coloured fruit. *Eugenia alba.*
Jatayu	King of birds and Dasaratha's friend – he belongs to the family of Garuda. While trying to save Sita from Ravana his wings are broken and he falls to the ground. He narrates the incident to Rama dies.
Jhau	A coniferous tree. *Tamarix indicus.*
Jhumkolata	'Jhumka' is an ornament worn in the ears. This name is also given to citron-leaved passion flower *Passiflora citrifolia* from the supposed resemblance of its flowers to the 'jhumka'.
Kaalapani	Literally, black waters. Refers to the sea.
Kabiraj	An ayurvedic doctor.
Kachu	The genetic name of *Arum*, several species of which are cultivated and eaten in different parts of the Indian subcontinent.
Kalojaam	See 'jaam'.
Kalia	Spicy fish curry popular in Bengal.

Kalidas	The reference is to the greatest of Sanskrit poets, known for his *Abhijnanasakuntalam* and *Meghadutam*. The yaksha mistakes the name for one of his relatives.
Kamranga	A sour fruit, often made into a *chutney*.
Kankan	Bracelet.
Kantikari	A herb or plant.
Kanshi	A dish of bell-metal used as a musical instrument.
Kayasthas	The second tier in the fourfold caste system—a non-priestly warrior caste.
Kekara	A woman with a squint.
Khadam	Rudimentary wooden slippers.
Khair	A tree that yields a gummy resin. *Acacia atechu*.
Khalassi	Sailor, dock worker or porter.
Khataash	Wild cat
Khatia	Charpoy. A stringed cot with a wooden frame.
Khel Khatam	An expression that means 'Finished!'.
Khoi	Popped rice.
Khoka	Young boy.
Kisti-toupee	A type of cap.
Krosh	A unit of distance equal to two miles.
Kupi	A small oil lamp. It is rudimentary in nature and can consist merely of a tin can containing the oil and a wick.

Kush	A kind of grass considered 'holy'. Worshippers sit on kush mats during a holy rite.
Laat Saheb	A wealthy gentleman (generally used for a person who does not need to work, or who thinks he does not need to!).
Lota	Water pot. A small tumbler.
Loochi	A round eatable made of dough, kneaded, rolled and then fried.
Mahua	A large tree from the flower of which an intoxicating liquor, also called *Mahua*, is distilled.
Mashi	Mother's sister. The Bangla term is more specific than the English 'aunt' and is more concise than 'mother's sister'; therefore, we have retained 'mashi' in the text.
Mashaal	A flaming torch.
Maurala	A tiny fresh-water fish
Maydanab	A monster and an artist. In the *Mahabharata* during *Khandabdaha*, Arjuna protected him. To repay his debt he built a magnificent court for the Pandavas in Indraprastha.
Mehrbani	Grace.
Mejo Serang	A rank in the sailor community. 'Mejo' implies 'second', i.e., not senior. The equivalent of serang would be 'bosun'.
Mirikin mulk	'Mulk' means land. In this story, 'American' is pronounced 'Mirikin'.

Mohanphuli	A sweet dish made of semolina.
Moorum	Small pebbles.
Moshai	A polite suffix attached to one's name or surname.
Muri	Puffed rice. It is a cheap and popular food item.
Nona-aata	A variety of custard-apple.
Natua	Amateur actor.
Nullah	A stream.
Ol	The root of *Arum campanulatum*. Select varieties are cooked and eaten.
Paan	Betel leaf.
Paara	An area or neighbourhood.
Paathshala	Village primary school.
Pe-lan	In the story, this is a mispronunciation of 'plan'.
Palo	Indigenous fishing equipment.
Phanimansa	A shrub, *Cactus indicus.*
Pidi	Short, wooden stool on which people sit, particularly during meals
Pindadaan	A funeral ritual for one's ancestors in Hindu tradition, often offered at Gaya in Bihar.
Poush	The ninth month of the Bengali calendar (from the middle of December to the middle of January).

Punya	Virtue. 'Punya' is a philosophical concept that can be aggregated ('purna arjan kora' in Bangla) through good deeds to compensate for the sins ('paap') one commits.
Rakshasi	A female rakshas (demon). A rakshasi (and a rakshas) eats human flesh.
Rudraksha	A fruit which is strung and used as holy beads.
Sabeda	A sweet fruit.
Sandhi Puja	Worship of Goddess Durga especially in autumn at the juncture of the eighth and the ninth lunar day.
Sankho ghanta	Conch and small hand-held gong used in Hindu ceremonies.
Sanyasi	Ascetic. One who has taken sanyas, i.e., one who has renounced the world.
Sarputi	A freshwater fish.
Shapla	A green-coloured water plant.
Shastra	Sacred Hindu law book.
Sheel	A stone slab used along with a grinding stone for grinding things.
Sindoor	Scarlet powder traditionally worn by married Hindu women on the parting in their hair.
Sooji	A preparation with semolina.
Sravan	The fourth month of the Bengali calendar (from the middle of July to the middle of August)

Supuri	Areca nut or betel nut.
Tabeez	Amulet worn by some Muslims.
Talapia	A medium-sized freshwater fish.
Taltola slippers	A particular kind of loose footwear which has almost become symbolic of the noveau riche 'babu' class of the late nineteenth and early twentieth centuries.
Taqlif	Trouble
Teensau Tees	330 (Hindi).
Teensau	300 (Hindi).
Thaala	A large plate.
Thaali	See Thaala
Thaan	A plain white piece of cloth some widows wear as sarees.
Tilak	A mark usually of ghee, chandan, (sandalwood paste) etc., put on one's forehead. Associated with Hinduism.
Tongighar	Aazan minaret.
Tvaya Hrisikesha	The reference is to Krishna, a reincarnation of Vishnu, in his capacity as lord of the senses
Unoon	A clay oven.
Yaksha	The spirit of a man which controls his possessions after death.
Yajmans	The clientele of Brahmin priests. A priest (and his successors) would carry out all the rituals required by the yajman.

Notes on Writers

Parashuram (1880-1960)

Rajsekhar Basu (Parashuram) wrote about a hundred stories from 1922 to1957. He used wit and humour to criticise society. He is often compared to Trailokyanath Mukhopadhyay, the great writer of satires in Bengal. Parashuram's humour has an urban touch and, is therefore, refined and sophisticated, although it lacks the energy and force of Trailokyanath. His writings are marked by a sharp and clear insight and a deft portrayal of characters. Among the more popular of his stories are, 'Sree Sree Siddeshwari Limited', 'Parashpathar', 'Kajjali', 'Hanumaner Swapna' and others.

Jagadish Gupta (1886-1957)

Jagadish Gupta turned away from romantic modes of writing and brought all the crudity, ferocity and harshness of reality to his stories. The helplessness of man in society and hidden forms of desire emerge as integral patterns in his works. A very powerful though not very popular writer, his short stories include, 'Puraton Bhritya', 'Bijoy Chakrabortyr Bikrom', 'Shashanko Kabirajer Stree' and others.

Banaphool (1899-1979)

Balaichand Mukhopadhyay wrote under the pen-name Banaphool. A doctor by profession, he drew from various spheres of knowledge and brought a rare craftsmanship to his stories. One encounters familiar characters from the everyday world in his stories written in a style marked by restraint. Banaphool is also known as the propagator of very short-stories. 'Nadi', 'Ajante', 'Neemgaach' and 'Manush' are among some of his better known stories.

Shibram Chakraborty (1902-1988)

During his school-life, Shibram Chakraborty was imprisoned for joining the Swadeshi movement. He started his literary career as a poet. But he soon made his mark as a very popular storyteller full of light-hearted humour. He explored the great resources of the language in the production of humour. He has about a hundred and fifty works to his credit. 'Prankestar Kirti', 'Burman Mama' and 'Labher Belai Ghanta', are among some of his popular stories.

Syed Mujtaba Ali (1904-1974)

Syed Mujtaba Ali's stories infuse life into the village backdrop while intricate details from everyday life contribute to a distinctive flavour to his stories. 'Ek Purush', 'Chachakahini' and 'Tunimem' are some of the better known ones.

Satinath Bhaduri (1906-1965)

Satinath Bhaduri's participation in the freedom movement, his imprisonment and his identification with the masses, found expression in his works. In the presentation of characters he provided his readers with new solutions to some essential problems. He is famous for the depiction of type characters in his short stories. The story 'Dakater Ma' was first published in

1954 in *Sharadiya Jugantar*. 'Gananayak', 'Banya', 'Dampatya Seemantey', and 'Patralekhar Baba' are some of his other stories.

Manik Bandyopadhyay (1908-1956)

Manik Bandyopadhyay (Prabodh Kumar) is one of the most prominent writers of the short story in Bangla. At the very onset of his writing career he discovered a social life and a time that were riddled with disease and death. As he advanced in life he consciously realized that a social upheaval and revolution were needed to rid society of its evils. In his writings we find a social analyst along with a sensitive narrator. Some of his well-known short stories include, 'Sareesrip', 'Pragaitihashik', 'Choto Bakulpurer Jatri', 'Tiktiki', and 'Haraner Natjammai'. He wrote about two hundred short stories.

Ashapurna Devi (1909-1995)

Ashapurna Devi is well known for her sensitive depiction of the everyday lives of women. She has an extraordinary eye for detail and a subtle and finely modulated style. She holds up a mirror as it were to both the inner and the outer lives of middle-class women. Some of her most prominent short stories are, 'Nabanna', 'Atmaja', 'Bhai' and 'Seemarekhar Seema'.

Subodh Ghose (1909-1980)

The author, along with Jagadish Gupta and Manik Bandyopadhyay, contributed to a distinctive change in the sphere of the short story coupled with a change in perspectives. Writing with a deep sense of social and economic reality, Subodh Ghose criticised the comfortable middle class with its split mentality. He rose to fame with the publication of 'Fossil', 'Sundaram' and 'Garal Amiya Bhel', published during the end of the World War II.

Jyotirindra Nandy (1912-1983)

The author used Jyotsna Ray as his pen-name in the early years of his writing. A story-teller following the tradition of Manik Bandyopadhyay, he became famous with his short story, 'Nadi O Nari'. His prose is marked by deep insights into the inner consciousness, a warmth of human emotions and a natural story-telling style. 'Palish', 'Abani Nikhoj', 'Jauban' and ' Arshola' are among some of his better known stories.

Narendranath Mitra (1917-1975)

Narendranath Mitra is the great artist of the dreams and aspirations, the joys and sorrows of the middle and the lower middle class. He reveals deep and unexpected complexities under the surface of a seemingly tranquil, middle-class life. The vision that one encounters is usually stoic for he offers no consolation. A few of his stories, like 'Mahanagar', 'Head Master' and 'Palanka' have been made into films.

Ramapada Chaudhuri b.1922

Ramapada Chaudhuri's early stories deal with life in Ranchi, Hazaribagh and Palamau. In his later stories, he concentrates on the urban middle-class experience, exploring modern themes. 'Darbari', 'Bharatvarsha', 'Chabi', 'Dinkal' and 'Dressing Table' are among some of his better known stories.

Narayan Gangopadhyay (1928-1985)

Narayan Gangopadhyay, also a theorist of the short story as genre, is one of the most important modern short story writers in Bengal. He believes in the realistic but symbolic nature of the short story and in the fact that experience has to undergo a total transformation in order to emerge as a story. Some of his popular stories are 'Koney Dekha Alo' 'Doshor' and 'Bitata Bitangsha'.

Dipendranath Bandyopadhyay (1933-1979)

Dwipendranath Bandyopadhyay brought a new dimension to the short story by introducing several innovative stylistic features. His stories depict a very intense world, somewhere between dream and reality but the dream world is in no way comfortable. His short story 'Jatayu' won him acclaim. 'Britto', 'Grohon' and 'Swayambar Sabha', are among some of his better known stories.

Moti Nandy b.1933

Moti Nandy brought a new sensibility to the world of short stories in Bengal. He won recognition with the publication of his short story, 'Behular Bhela' in 1958. Nandy often goes into new, unexplored areas for his themes – the world of games for instance. 'Behular Bhela', 'Phuldani', 'Ebong Tara Phire Elo' and 'Samanya Jeeban' are some of his well known short stories.